A HOLIDAY HAUNTING AT THE BILTMORE

THE MYSTERY HOUSE SERIES, BOOK EIGHT

Eva Pohler

Eva Pohler Books
20011 Park Ranch
San Antonio, Texas 78259
www.evapohler.com

Publisher's Note: This is a work of fiction. Names, characters, places, and incidents are a product of the author's imagination. Locales and public names are sometimes used for atmospheric purposes. Any resemblance to actual people, living or dead, or to businesses, companies, events, institutions, or locales is completely coincidental.

Copy Editor: Alexis Rigoni

Book Cover Design by B Rose DesignZ

A Holiday Haunting at the Biltmore/ Eva Pohler. -- 1st ed.
ISBN: 978-1-958390-31-3

Contents

For Zelda Fitzgerald, whose words were stolen and whose contributions to American literature were never acknowledged.

CHAPTER ONE

Hot Tub Musings

Ellen clung to the handrail as she eased down the steps into the hot, bubbling water. She adjusted her black one-piece bathing suit, making sure she was still covered. The aquafit class had rearranged everything.

From behind her, Sue said, "I can't believe I let you guys talk me into this."

"It wasn't that bad," Tanya said from where she was already resting in the tub.

Ellen sat across from her. "Speak for yourself. I could barely breathe."

Sue followed Ellen through the water, the ruffles of her polka-dotted bathing suit dancing on the surface. "I may have even died for a few minutes. I thought I saw a light at the end of a tunnel and my mother waving to me."

"That was probably just the Nazi instructor on deck telling you to lift your knees higher," Ellen teased.

Two other women from the aquafit class, both in their early seventies, joined Ellen and her friends.

"That instructor isn't as good as the one on Tuesdays," one of them, a petite woman with white hair, said. She was nearly as thin as Tanya.

The other woman, rounder than Ellen but not as round as Sue, nodded. "The one on Tuesday *really* works you."

"Oh, Lord." Sue pushed her dark brown bangs from her eyes. "Let's not come on Tuesday."

"We already agreed that we would," Tanya pointed out. "At least until the wedding."

Ellen tugged at her shoulder straps, trying to keep everything in the right place. "You can count on me. I'm determined to lose twenty pounds or die trying."

Sue scoffed. "Well, maybe I love life more than you."

"If that were true," the petite woman with the white hair began, "you'd keep coming. I've been doing this for over thirty years. I used to be bigger than both of you combined."

The woman pointed at Ellen and Sue. Ellen tried not to be offended. The audacity of some people, she thought.

"I'm sold!" Sue said comedically, lifting her finger high in the air. "Sign me up! Oh, that's right. Tanya already did."

The other women laughed, and Ellen's mood lightened.

"Did I hear you say that you have a wedding coming up?" the rounder woman asked Tanya.

"Not my wedding," Tanya said as her blue eyes widened. "It's Ellen's son. He's getting married on Christmas eve at the Biltmore Estate."

"Oh, how nice," the petite woman said. "That's the most beautiful house in the country."

Ellen leaned against the lip of the tub and breathed in the smell of lavender and musk. "That's what my son's future in-laws say, too. They've been planning this wedding since their daughter was a baby, I think."

"Are they from Asheville then?" the petite one asked.

"They live there," Sue said. Then, turning to Ellen, she asked, "Is it the mother who's related to the Vanderbilts?"

"Yes," Ellen said.

"Which means they're getting the works," Sue gloated. "The entire wedding party and their guests will be staying at the Biltmore House, which is never done anymore."

Ellen gave Sue her keep-your-mouth-shut look. Maya's parents had asked them not to talk about the event with others. They wanted to avoid a media circus.

"How wonderful," the petite woman said. "You sure you don't need another grandmother to come?"

Ellen smiled but said nothing in reply.

"That sounds like a once-in-a-lifetime experience." The round woman climbed from the tub. "I hope you enjoy it, and have a nice weekend, ladies."

"You, too," Ellen said as Sue and Tanya waved.

"I should go, too," the petite woman said. "Will I see you all on Tuesday?"

"We'll be here." Tanya turned to Sue. "Right?"

Sue shrugged. "We shall see."

After the two women left, and she and her friends were alone in the hot tub, Ellen said, "Poor Lane is so stressed over this wedding."

"I thought that was the job of the bride," Sue said.

Tanya stood up. "It can be hard on the groom, too. Poor thing. What's been the most stressful for him?"

Ellen sighed. "Maya's grandparents. Both sets are still alive, and, apparently, one set can't stand the other, and vice versa."

Sue furrowed her brows. "Do you know why?"

"Lane doesn't know the whole story. The grandfathers were friends long before Maya's parents were born. According to Maya, they can be really nasty when forced to be in the same room."

"That's too bad," Tanya said as she took her damp blonde hair from its ponytail, and then remade it higher on her head. "I hope they won't ruin the wedding."

Ellen's stomach clenched. She wanted Lane's wedding day to be perfect for him so that only happy memories would be made.

"I would think the setting alone would be enough to sweeten even the sourest grapes of the bunch," Sue said reassuringly.

Ellen lifted her brows. "I hope you're right."

"Is it Maya's maternal grandfather or grandmother that's related to the Vanderbilts?" Tanya asked.

Ellen submerged to her neck. She let out a small gasp of pleasure as the hot water relaxed her muscles, tight from the workout. Then she said, "Grandmother. Melissa Dresden—used to be Brown. She's the daughter to a cousin of George Vanderbilt, the one who made it all happen. I just read a book about it called *The Last Castle* by Denise Kiernan. It was interesting to read about the estate's history. George fell in love with Asheville when he took his ailing mother there to breathe."

"To *what*?" Tanya asked.

"To breathe," Ellen repeated. "Back then, they believed fresh air was the cure for almost everything—especially tuberculosis—and Asheville had become known for its breathing porches that overlooked the beautiful Blue Ridge and Smoky Mountains."

"George's mother had tuberculosis?" Sue asked. "Most people didn't survive it."

"No, she had malaria, and she recovered from it, but not before George fell in love with the area and began buying up all the land."

"What year was this?" Tanya asked.

"Late 1800s," Ellen said. "According to the book, George wasn't interested in the family business like his two older brothers, who took over various railroad companies when their father died. George was more of a scholar. He loved to read and to collect art, and he wanted something different for himself. So, he decided to outdo his siblings by building the largest private home in America."

Sue nodded. "That he did."

"It was more than that, though, wasn't it?" Tanya asked. "Didn't he build a famous dairy?"

"Yes—though now it's a winery. He also hired the best forester and horticulturalist and created a forest preserve and foresters' school. Later, his wife Edith, who outlived him by many years, created a school for the villagers that focused on textiles and crafts, I believe. Apparently, Edith did a lot for Asheville. I think she was the real heart of Biltmore, only because George died young. They had a daughter named Cornelia, but, according to the book, she was never as devoted to Biltmore as her mother."

"How old was George when he died?" Sue asked.

"Early fifties, I think. Younger than us."

"Can you believe I turn sixty next year?" Tanya asked.

"Already?" Sue covered her face with her hands. "I'm right behind you."

"Brian's sixty-two, and he's fine," Ellen pointed out. "It's not the end of the world."

"Not yet, anyway," Sue said.

"That's too bad about Maya's grandparents," Tanya said. "I really hope they behave themselves at the wedding."

"Me, too." Ellen sighed and leaned back on the lip of the tub. "Lane says that Maya's Vanderbilt grandmother was originally engaged to Maya's other grandfather, and that's why the two sets of grandparents don't get along. One man stole the Vanderbilt bride from the other."

"Must be hard for the grandmother who isn't a Vanderbilt," Sue pointed out. "She might feel like chopped liver. Don't you think?"

"I know I would, in her situation," Tanya said. "How selfish of her husband that he can't let it go."

"Lane doesn't think that's the whole story," Ellen said. "I just hope they can be civil for the sake of their granddaughter."

"And for the rest of us," Tanya added.

Sue shrugged. "I don't know. Drama at the Biltmore might be fun."

"Don't say that," Ellen insisted. "I'm worried enough about the other encounters we may have while we're there."

"Did the book say the house is haunted?" Tanya asked.

"No, and when I asked the Biltmore wedding coordinator about it, she said that they weren't allowed to discuss it."

"It's rumored to be." Sue furrowed her brows again. "And if Biltmore employees have been warned against talking about it, then you know what that means."

Tanya stretched her arms. "It's a good thing we're taking along some of our equipment."

"I'm afraid not to," Ellen said. "Ghosts have a way of finding us, and I don't want to be caught unprepared."

"They find us because we have the gift, and they can sense it," Sue said.

"What do Lane and Maya think about it?" Tanya climbed up and sat on the edge of the tub with her legs in the water.

"I haven't mentioned it to them," Ellen admitted. "I'd like to keep any ghostly happenings away from the wedding, as much as possible."

"Have you done any research, to learn if anyone has written about hauntings there?" Sue asked.

Ellen combed her fingers through her short, damp hair. "I've read about ghosts in Asheville, but very little is said about hauntings at the Biltmore. One book claimed that George Vanderbilt's ghost is there."

"I wonder what unfinished business a billionaire would have, that would keep him from moving on," Tanya said.

Ellen climbed up and sat beside Tanya. "Hopefully, it's only a rumor, and the wedding will go off without a hitch—worldly or otherwise."

"I'm sure it will," Tanya reassured her.

"We'll find out in two months' time," Sue said. "That is, if we survive Aquafit."

Ellen and Tanya looked at each other and grinned.

CHAPTER TWO

Grove Park Inn and the Pink Lady

The flight into Asheville was too bumpy for Ellen. She clutched Brian's hand and tried to keep from getting sick. Tanya, across the aisle from her beside Sue, didn't look much better.

"We're nearly there," Brian reassured Ellen, his gray eyes bright.

She turned to Lane and Maya in the seats behind them, the smell of peppermint wafting from someone's chewing gum. "You two doing okay?"

"We're fine, Mom," Lane replied. "But you don't look so good. I have Dramamine if you need it."

"I'll be alright."

"Can I have some Dramamine?" Tanya asked Lane.

"I got you."

As Lane climbed from his seat, Ellen said, "I'm not sure it's safe to stand up right now."

"I'll be fine." He opened the overhead compartment and fished through his carry-on luggage for the medicine. Then he handed it to Tanya before returning to his seat.

"Thanks so much," Tanya said.

"How's Sue?" Ellen asked Tanya.

Sue bent forward to meet Ellen's gaze. "I'm just peachy. But remind me what the dinner plans are for tonight. I know we have the rehearsal dinner tomorrow, but . . . You did say we were invited to the rehearsal dinner, right?"

"I changed my mind," Ellen said. "You and Tanya will have to fend for yourselves."

"She's joshing you," Lane said. "Of course, you're invited—your hubbies, too."

"Tom won't make it in time," Sue said. "He won't arrive until Saturday morning with Luke, Lexi, and Stephen."

"Dave won't either," Tanya said. "And Mike, Seth, and Cammie are flying up on Friday night, but too late for the rehearsal dinner."

"That's when Nolan, Taylor, and Alison are coming," Ellen said. "I wonder if they're on the same flight."

"Probably," Tanya said.

"I was worried about Taylor flying," Ellen said, "with her being pregnant and all, but Nolan insists it's fine."

"He is a doctor," Tanya said. "He should know. Are they bringing Brianna?"

"They thought about leaving her with Taylor's parents," Ellen said, "but decided against it, since it's Christmas. Last year, when we flew to Montana, she did great."

"But she was an infant then," Brian pointed out. "It might not be as easy now that she can talk."

"How old is she?" Tanya asked.

"Almost two," Ellen said with a smile. "And I can't wait to see her."

"Now that we have that sorted," Sue continued, "are there any plans for tonight? Or do we need to fend for ourselves?"

"Maya and I plan to take it easy," Lane said. "We'll probably order room service and destress, right, babe?"

"Yes, please," Maya said, her brown eyes looking tired. "We didn't even tell my parents that we're flying in tonight. They think we're arriving in the morning." She leaned against Lane's shoulder and closed her eyes.

"You two aren't sharing a room, are you?" Sue asked with disbelief. "Isn't it bad luck?"

Lane grinned. "That's just something the old heads made up to keep the young heads in line until after marriage."

Ellen guffawed.

Sue shook her head and leaned back in her seat while Tanya swallowed her Dramamine. Ellen closed her eyes and hoped the plane would stop jolting.

"Don't worry, Sue," Brian said. "We've got reservations at the Edison tonight."

"As long as there's a plan," she said. "That's all I need to know."

The Omni Grove Park Inn sat wedged in the Blue Ridge Mountains overlooking acres of landscaped and natural gardens—including a golf course. It was breathtaking to Ellen as she sat with Brian and her two best friends and her son and his bride in the shuttle. The late afternoon sun was just beginning its western descent as the shuttle began its climb uphill toward the grand hotel. It was as large as any castle. Built of stone in the arts and crafts style with a red tiled roof, the hotel was the only edifice the eye could see in the vicinity. Several natural trees along the exterior of the building were decorated for Christmas.

Ellen sat up in her seat. "Isn't it beautiful?"

"I wasn't expecting this," Tanya said, returning Ellen's smile. "I knew the Biltmore would be amazing, but I wasn't expecting the inn to be, too. Just wow."

"It's stunning," Brian agreed.

"Lots of famous people have stayed here," Ellen said. "Lots of presidents, including Obama . . . and let's see . . . F. Scott Fitzgerald . . . "

"He wrote *The Great Gatsby*, right?" Brian lifted his brows.

"Right," Sue said.

"That's why Ellen fell in love with me," Brian teased. "Because I know a thing or two about literature."

"She told me it was your backside," Sue said with a grin.

"It was his eyes," Ellen said, blushing. Those gray eyes and dark brows mesmerized her. "Not that there's anything wrong with his backside."

"I don't mind—either way," Brian said with a laugh.

Ellen shook her head and grinned. "Anyway, this is also where people have claimed to have seen the Pink Lady—a ghost in a pink ball gown. I read about it in one of my Asheville books."

"Did it say why she hasn't moved on?" Tanya asked as the shuttle neared the magnificent, stacked-stone façade.

"Uh-uh. She was just some young woman who either jumped or fell several stories over the banister during a 1920's ball in the Palm Court. It was a mystery then, and it's a mystery now."

"How intriguing," Sue said. "Maybe we should reach out to her tonight."

"Let's play it by ear." Ellen glanced toward the back seat, where Lane and Maya sat. "I don't want to forget the real reason why we're here."

"Don't worry about us," Lane insisted. "As I said before, we're just going to crash in our room tonight and rest up for the big days ahead."

Once inside the expansive but dimly lit lobby, which smelled of cinnamon and citrus, they discovered more elaborate Christmas décor, including a life-size gingerbread house near the entrance to the Sunset Terrace. Throughout the rustic, stone-clad lobby, flanked by two massive stone fireplaces, were tabletop exhibits of edible gingerbread houses. Some of them had ribbons beside them indicating first, second, and third place, along with honorable mentions.

"These are incredible," Sue said as she walked around one of the tables eyeing the various creations.

Ellen and the others followed, admiring in miniature a chuck wagon, a carousel, Santa's sleigh, panda bears playing flutes, a pirate ship, elves riding giraffes, and dozens of other gingerbread inventions.

"I had no idea about this," Maya said. "What a pleasant surprise."

"I guess it's a good thing the Biltmore House is only available to us during the night of the wedding," Ellen said. "We would have missed this altogether."

"True," Brian said. "Check this one out. What does it remind you of?"

Ellen smiled. Brian had taken her to Paris during their honeymoon, and the gingerbread house was a replica of the Louvre Museum, where they had shared a special day.

"What is it?" Lane asked.

"The Louvre in Paris," Ellen replied.

"It has a lot in common architecturally with the Biltmore," Maya said.

"I suppose it would." Tanya leaned over the gingerbread house. "They were both built in the style of the French chateau."

Ellen often forgot that Tanya had studied abroad in France as a graduate student and knew the language and culture well.

"Smarty pants," Sue teased.

"They look beautiful and delicious," Ellen said.

Sue put her hands on her hips. "Do you think anyone would miss it if I took off with this Eiffel Tower?"

Ellen and the others laughed.

"Probably," Brian said with a chuckle. "Look. There's a bar over there."

A couple sat together on barstools sharing what looked like chocolate lava cake with cherries. Ellen's mouth began to water as she realized how hungry she was. They hadn't eaten since breakfast, and it was way past lunchtime.

Just then, Ellen noticed Maya gaping at an older couple entering the lobby. The man was tall, robust, and bald, and the woman was the opposite—barely five feet, thin, with gorgeous, thick, white hair that flowed to her shoulders.

"Grandma? Grandpa?" Maya cried with a look of excitement.

"Oh, it's Maya!" the thin woman said, beaming.

Ellen watched as her future daughter-in-law rushed across the lobby and into her grandmother's arms. The tall, robust grandfather, who reminded Ellen of Mr. Clean, enfolded them both and kissed Maya on the cheek. Ellen wondered if they were the Vanderbilt grandparents, whose surname was Dresden, or the Stones. If she remembered correctly, the Dresdens resided in Asheville, so these must be the Stones. The petite woman with the long, white hair and gorgeous brown eyes—eyes that Maya had clearly inherited—must be the chopped liver.

Later that evening, after an early dinner with Maya's grandparents—a surprisingly lovely couple—Ellen, Sue, and Tanya joined Brian on the Sunset Terrace to watch the sun's descent behind the Blue Ridge Mountains while they sipped on hot coffee with Baileys Irish Cream. It was too chilly to remain on the terrace for more than fifteen minutes, so once the spectacular show was over, they returned to the lobby, also known as the Great Hall, and sat on rocking chairs in front of one of the tall stone fireplaces. A cozy fire crackled in the hearth and made the space smell like roasted chestnuts. There was a beautifully decorated Christmas tree next to the fireplace that gave the expansive room a cozy, cheerful feel despite the many other guests also lounging about.

"If Gayle Stone is chopped liver," Sue began, "then I'm a monkey's uncle. I've never met a more beautiful and pleasant woman her age."

"Should Tom be jealous?" Brian asked with a twinkle in his gray eyes.

Sue chuckled. "I'd forgotten how funny you can be."

"I'm just trying to keep up with you," he said, full of charm.

"Ted seemed nice, too," Tanya put in. "It's hard to imagine them in a decades-long fued with the other set of grandparents."

"I agree." Ellen took another sip of the delicious, hot coffee.

"Do we still want to attempt to talk to the Pink Lady tonight?" Sue wondered. "Or are you guys too tired?"

Brian kissed Ellen on the cheek. "That's my cue to leave."

"You're welcome to join us." Ellen squeezed his hand.

"Thanks, love, but I have an early tee time, so I might as well turn in."

"Who are you playing with?" Sue asked.

"Just me and my lonesome. I promised Mike and Tom that I'd play with them Saturday morning, though, so consider this my practice round."

"Mike plays golf?" Sue asked Tanya with her brows pressed together.

"Not my Mike," Tanya said. "Brian's brother."

"Oh, your brother's coming?" Sue asked. "Will he be bringing the whole family?"

"Just Marcia," Brian said. "The rest of their tribe has gotten too big to coordinate."

Brian leaned over and kissed Ellen on the lips before heading to the elevator behind the fireplace. She felt a wave of déjà vu. Although Brian played every so often with clients and associates, Paul used to play every weekend. All this talk of turning in for an early tee time had reminded her of him.

She knew why Brian had made the tee time—to give her space. He was trying not to smother her while they continued to find their footing as newlyweds. As much as she appreciated his efforts, she hoped he would enjoy himself, too.

"We aren't going to do our séance here in the lobby, are we?" Tanya asked. "Why don't we go to my room? We need our equipment anyway."

"Hold that elevator, Brian!" Sue cried as the three friends jumped to their feet and followed him.

Ellen and her friends decided to take a few inconspicuous tools with them to the Palm Court, the original lobby located on the third floor, where the Pink Lady reportedly fell to her death. Fortunately, there were only two other people there—a young couple nestled close together on the opposite end of the room from where Ellen, Tanya, and Sue took their seats. Ellen could barely see them on the other side of a large potted palm—one of six for which the room had been named.

They took some initial readings with a thermometer and EMF detector. Although they hadn't brought their bulkier equipment, they had two new tools Ellen was anxious to try: a REM-POD and a ghost box app.

As Ellen pulled the REM-POD, a plastic device about four inches in diameter and height, from her should bag, Tanya asked, "How does that work again?"

"The REM-POD radiates electromagnetic energy around it, to feed the spirits, and this antenna picks up on anything that touches it or comes within an inch of it from any angle."

Ellen turned it on. As soon as her finger was within an inch of the antenna, the device made a beep, and a yellow light went off. She glanced at the couple behind her as they were getting up to leave.

"I hope I didn't scare you off," Ellen called to them with an apologetic smile.

"We were ready to head back anyway," the young man said. "Good night."

"Good night," Sue said with a wave.

"And what about that app on your phone?" Tanya asked.

"It works like a ghost box." Ellen handed her phone to Tanya. "Go ahead and turn it on."

Tanya tapped the button on Ellen's phone.

"Radio static?" Tanya asked.

Sue cocked her head to the side. "Haven't you heard of a ghost box?"

Tanya frowned. "I thought we didn't believe in them."

"I know," Ellen said. "I'm still skeptical but thought we should give it a try. The app shuffles white noise from radio frequencies."

"How can a spirit control what words come through?" Tanya asked, still frowning.

"We don't have to use it." Ellen took back her phone. "Let's just give the REM-POD a try, okay?"

"I mean, we can try both of them if you want," Tanya said. "I just wouldn't base the investigation on data from that app."

"It can be supplemental data," Sue said. "Okay?"

Tanya nodded. Ellen didn't really care whether they used the app. She felt confident in their abilities with or without it.

"Are you wearing your *gris gris*?" Ellen asked.

Each revealed the small bag tied to a thin leather cord, worn around the neck beneath the blouse.

"Good," Ellen said. "I'll just sprinkle a little salt—not a circle, but just a little for extra protection."

Not wanting to make a mess, Ellen sprinkled the salt so lightly that most of it fell into the carpet piles and wasn't visible.

"We might not have any luck without candles," Sue said. "Are you sure you don't want to risk it?"

"I'm sure," Ellen said. "I don't want to get us kicked out. We have to put Lane and Maya first."

"Of course," Sue said. "You're right."

"We could always try the Ouija Board," Tanya said.

"Better not do that here," Ellen said, not wanting to do anything that might put Lane's big day in jeopardy.

Tanya clicked her tongue. "It's funny to me how people will use all these other tools without batting an eye, but they believe the Ouija Board will make you more vulnerable to evil spirits."

"I believe it does make us more vulnerable," Sue said. "And I've learned recently that we haven't been opening and closing it safely. You have to say goodbye. Did you know that?"

Ellen shrugged. "No. But okay, we can do that. Why do you think it makes us more vulnerable, Sue?"

"Because it's an instrument of the occult," she said.

"But so is this nimrod," Tanya said.

Ellen laughed. "REM-POD."

Sue shook her head. "But the Ouija Board is an ancient tool of the occult. These modern devices are things we use every day—electricity and cameras and thermometers."

Tanya rolled her eyes. "I don't know if I agree."

"I'm not against using the Ouija Board," Sue said. "In fact, I'm pretty sure that I was the one that first got us using it if memory serves. I just think it has to be handled more carefully than our other tools—that's all."

"Let's get started," Ellen said. "Ready?"

The others nodded as they took one another's hands.

"Should I begin?" Ellen asked.

"You don't always have to be the leader," Sue pointed out.

"Then you go," Ellen insisted. "I forgot how much you enjoy being our queen."

"Don't envy me," Sue teased. "Heavy is the head that wears the crown."

Ellen put her hands on her hips. "You stole that from *Downton Abbey*."

"Yes, I did," Sue said with a laugh. "Anyway, maybe Tanya wants to lead."

Tanya shook her head. "I'm good."

"Alright, then." Sue closed her eyes and lifted her chin. "Spirits of the other realm, we come in peace. We want to help, not harm. Negative energy or evil spirits are not allowed to communicate with us. We are seeking the one known as the Pink Lady. If you're here, can you give us a sign? You can use our instruments to feed yourself the energy you need to communicate with us."

Ellen let go of Sue's hand and reached over to touch the small, round REM-POD near her feet, causing it to beep. Tanya jumped nearly a foot out of her chair.

"Sorry," Ellen whispered. Then more loudly, she said, "You can touch this device to make a noise, showing us that you're here with us."

"Or you can knock, or, if possible, speak to us," Sue added, as she took Ellen's hand again.

The women waited in silence for about thirty seconds before Tanya said, "Maybe she's not here."

"Do you smell that?" Ellen whispered.

The odor of rotten eggs wafted through the courtyard. Ellen wrinkled her nose.

"Tanya, you shouldn't have had the garlic roll at dinner," Sue teased.

"Oh, stop," Tanya said.

Suddenly, the REM-POD beeped, and the yellow light blinked, and this time Ellen nearly jumped from her seat.

"Was that you, Ellen?" Sue asked, opening her eyes.

Ellen shook her head, her heart beating fast.

Sue swallowed hard. "If the Pink Lady is here with us now, please touch the REM-POD again."

Another beep.

Ellen and her friends stared at one another with their eyes and mouths wide open.

Sue took a deep breath. "Would you like to speak to us today, Pink Lady? If so, touch the REM-POD again."

Silence.

"Maybe she doesn't want to talk to us," Tanya whispered.

At that moment, Ellen caught a flash of pink about the size of a laptop swirl past her legs, from the REM-POD to the other side of the room.

"Did you see that?" she asked.

Tanya nodded, unable to speak.

Sue furrowed her brows. "See what?"

Sue looked around, trying to follow Ellen and Tanya's gaze. She turned to look over her shoulder and froze.

It was a blur of pink swaying and shimmering near the wall behind Sue. Ellen's hands and knees shook as adrenaline surged through her, reminding her of how excited she felt while investigating the paranormal. To think that she and her friends had almost given this up.

"Why is she here if she doesn't want to speak to us?" Tanya wondered out loud.

Ellen squinted as the shimmering pink blur took on the form of a young woman in a beautiful gown. Ellen gasped and her heart raced. She heard Tanya's sudden intake of air, too, and felt the hair on the back of her own neck rise. A cold chill filled the room.

She let go of her friends' hands, took out her phone, and opened the ghost box app, which immediately made static sounds—white noise.

"If you have something to say to us," she began, "you could use this device to choose words from the different radio frequencies."

Although the apparition vanished, Ellen nearly dropped her phone when the words, "I want," came over loud and clear.

The three friends glanced at one another with excitement.

"What do you want?" Sue asked.

"To be," the ghost box app said.

Tanya's face went white. "Maybe she wants to be left alone."

Then a moment later, the app said, "Seen."

One of the overhead lights flickered and went out.

"She wants to be seen," Sue repeated.

"We saw you," Ellen said. "You looked beautiful."

And it was true. Her face had been young, her figure slight, and her smile attractive. Only her red eyes and her translucence had made her distinct from a living person.

The ghost box app said, "He wanted."

"Who wanted what?" Sue asked.

"Jonathon."

"Who's Jonathon?" Ellen asked.

"Lover."

"Her lover?" Tanya wondered.

"Keep me," the app said.

"Keep me?" Ellen repeated with confusion.

"Hidden," the app said. "I wanted."

"You wanted to be seen?" Sue asked glancing at her friends before turning back to the apparition.

"Yes. So . . . he . . . pushed me."

The three friends gasped at once.

"Maybe her lover was married," Tanya speculated, "and he pushed her to keep her from telling his wife."

The ghost app startled them again when it said, "Yes."

"What's your name?" Sue asked.

A couple emerged from the elevator, and when they saw Ellen and her friends with their equipment, they stopped short.

"What's going on?" the young man asked.

From the ghost app came the words: "I want . . . to be . . . seen . . . I . . . want to . . . be seen . . . I want to . . . be . . . seen."

The young couple returned to the elevator and left the floor.

Alone again, Sue asked, "Are you still here?"

The app said, "Yes."

Then Tanya asked, "Wouldn't you like to go to the other side and find peace? Wouldn't you like to leave this place and join your departed loved ones?"

Again, the ghost app said, "I want . . . to . . . be seen . . . I want . . . to . . . be seen."

"She doesn't want to leave," Tanya mumbled.

"Yes," the ghost box app said.

"What's your name?" Ellen asked.

As they waited for a reply, they listened to static from the ghost box app. It seemed to Ellen that nearly a minute had gone by while they sat there, just breathing and listening.

"Are you still there?" Sue finally asked.

More static.

"Hello?" Ellen asked.

They waited for several more seconds, but nothing else came over the app.

Tanya sighed. "I think she left. That was so cool."

"It really was," Ellen agreed.

Sue waved her phone at them. "It's dead. It was at seventy-five percent when we sat down, and now it's dead."

"I guess I was wrong about the ghost box app," Tanya said. "That sounded pretty reliable to me."

"We just solved the mystery of the Pink Lady," Ellen said beaming. "She was the mistress of a married man who kept her a secret. She wanted to go to the ball and be with him openly. So, he pushed her."

"And she haunts this hotel because she still wants to be seen," Sue added.

Ellen took a deep breath, trying to calm her shaking hands. "I guess not every ghost wants to move on, and we have to accept that."

"Why don't we celebrate our success with one of those chocolate lava cakes with cherries?" Sue suggested. "We could split it."

"Count me in," Tanya said.

They looked questioningly at Ellen.

"I need to fit into my dress for the wedding."

"One lava cake won't change anything," Sue said.

"That's how it starts, though," Ellen said.

"How what starts?" Tanya wondered.

"The road to hell: one lava cake at a time."

The three women laughed but knew good and well that they would buy their cake and eat it, too.

<u>CHAPTER THREE</u>

Something in the Pool

The next morning after breakfast, Ellen, Sue, and Tanya headed downstairs to the subterranean spa. Ellen had read in one of her Asheville books that it was the best in the nation, so she was looking forward to it.

They checked in with the receptionist—a young woman in her twenties with her dark hair pulled back in a bun—who then led them to the women's locker room. First, they entered a cozy, carpeted lounging area with a stone fireplace, a couch, wingback chairs, and a coffee table with magazines. The air smelled like lemons and rosemary. They followed the receptionist through the area to the lockers.

"You'll find robes and fresh towels in there," the receptionist said, opening one of the lockers. "Program the locks by pressing 'key' and a four-digit number. Then press 'key' again. Do the same thing to unlock them. Slippers are in the pockets of your robe."

"How fancy," Tanya said.

"Before you change, let me give you a tour."

The receptionist took them from the lockers to the showers, the toilets, and another sitting room where there was hot water and herbal tea bags, along with cream and sugar and light snacks. There was also a big pitcher of iced water and glassware.

"Just don't take the glasses into the spa areas."

The receptionist then led them to a colorful whirlpool tub that was inside the women's locker room. A waterfall added luxury to the bubbling water. Ellen was surprised that there was no one else there.

"Clothing is optional in here, as well as in the eucalyptus steam and sauna rooms, for ladies only," the receptionist said. "But once you go through those doors to the coed area, we ask that you wear either your robe or a bathing suit—no nudity there, please."

"Oh, darn," Sue teased.

The receptionist then led them to the coed spa, where several people were relaxing in the pools and in loungers on the deck.

The main pool was shaped like a clover with a fireplace on the opposite wall lightly veiled by a waterfall. There were thick round columns of stacked stones rising from the pool where the clover leaves intersected. Sconces on the columns added soft light overhead. Above, skylights allowed some of the morning sun to shine past stone arcs and steel beams. Underwater fiberoptics in greens, blues, and reds emanated a magical atmosphere.

Two hot tubs on either side of the main pool had waterfalls cascading down walls of stacked stone.

"I've never been more eager to get undressed," Sue said as they followed the receptionist back to the women's locker room.

Ellen shook her head and giggled.

"Once you've changed into your robe," the receptionist began, "have a seat by the fireplace and your massage therapist will be with you shortly."

As they changed behind wooden screens, Ellen said, "I was tempted to try one of the bikini waxes. Have either of you ever had that done?"

"Not me," Tanya said. "It sounds too painful."

"Me neither," Sue said, "though I noticed on the menu that you can have it done in different shapes—like the Bermuda triangle, the power strip, the heart, and the arrow."

"The power strip?" Tanya asked laughing. "Like with outlets?"

"It depends on who you want to plug in," Sue said with a chuckle.

"Oh, gosh," Ellen said. "I wonder how many women Brian has been with that had neat little shapes like that. Maybe I should do it."

"Well, if I *did* do it," Sue began, "I think I'd ask for a yield sign, or, better yet, a stop sign."

Ellen and Tanya laughed.

Once they were in their robes and had their clothes and purses locked up, they sat by the fire to await their massage therapists.

Tanya picked up a magazine. "I think I'll get another Brazilian blow-out after this, because I don't want to worry about keeping my hair dry."

"The steam room will curl it up for sure," Ellen pointed out.

Sue giggled. "That reminds me of my mother-in-law. She had one done a few years ago for the holidays, but she kept calling it a Brazilian blowjob."

Ellen guffawed. "Oh, my gosh!"

"She even told Lexi, 'You need to get yourself a Brazilian blowjob.' She said it in front of the whole family! Lexi was mortified."

Tanya covered her mouth. "I would have been, too."

One by one, their massage therapists came and took them to a private room. Tanya and Sue had opted for a hand, foot, and scalp massage. Ellen had asked for the works, so by the time she was finished and had changed into her bathing suit, her friends were already waiting for her in the whirlpool of the ladies' locker room.

"How was it?" Ellen climbed into the hot bubbling water with them.

"Wonderful," Sue said. "Yours?"

"Fabulous."

Tanya blushed. "I think I scared my therapist."

Ellen lifted her brows. "What? How?"

Sue giggled. "I've already heard the story. I had to talk Tanya into staying. She wanted to leave."

"What? Why?"

"Well," Tanya began. "She kept asking me to tell her if she was pressing too hard. She didn't seem very confident. I just wanted to relax, but she kept saying, 'I'm sorry. Is that too hard?' and I would say, 'It's okay. It feels good.' I said this over and over, trying to reassure her. Well, while she was working up my leg, her hand slipped, and she hit my, you know, private area."

"Oops," Ellen giggled.

Tanya blushed. "I kept my eyes closed and wished she would pretend it hadn't happened, but instead she said, 'I'm so sorry.' And because I'd been saying it repeatedly, I said, 'It's okay. It feels good.'"

Ellen and Sue busted out laughing as Tanya's face turned the color of a fire engine.

"Who knows?" Ellen said when she could speak again. "Maybe she liked that you liked it."

Tanya rolled her eyes.

"She may have even done it on purpose," Ellen teased again.

"Oh, stop," Tanya said.

Changing the subject, Ellen said, "Okay enough of that. I can't wait to see the Biltmore Estate. The photos online looked amazing."

"It's supposed to be especially beautiful at Christmas." Sue leaned her head back on the edge of the pool, the rest of her body rising to the surface.

"I hope Lane is ready for this," Ellen said with a sigh.

"What makes you think otherwise?" Tanya asked.

Ellen shrugged. "I know he loves Maya—there's no question about that. It's just that, well, Nolan had his career figured out and a job secured before he proposed to Taylor. Lane just graduated and still doesn't know what he wants to do."

"I thought he was painting for commissions and producing his own music," Sue said.

"He is, but he still needs something stable."

"Didn't you say Maya got a job with an accounting firm in San Antonio?" Tanya asked.

"Yes. She's all set. It's Lane I'm worried about."

"With Maya's salary and her family money, along with the money from the oil, I really don't think you have much to worry about," Sue said. "Lane will be just fine."

"He's thinking about landscaping now," Ellen said. "Oh, I know he'll be fine. I just want him to be happy."

"He seems really, really happy with Maya," Tanya said.

Ellen smiled and laid back, floating like Sue. The hot water relaxed her neck and shoulders—the areas where she seemed to carry her stress. She had just closed her eyes when she felt something against her foot. Thinking it was just Sue or Tanya, she ignored it.

But a few moments later, a hand wrapped around her ankle.

"Cut it out," she said without opening her eyes.

"Cut what out?" Sue asked.

Ellen looked at Sue. "Is that you, grabbing my foot?"

Tanya and Sue glanced at one another with puzzled expressions.

"Something grabbed your foot?" Tanya asked.

Ellen still thought they were messing with her, so she said nothing more. She resumed her position but kept her eyes opened.

As before, she felt a hand wrap around her ankle. Sue and Tanya weren't close enough to be the culprits.

The hair on the back of her neck prickled.

"Guys," she whispered, but her friends couldn't hear her over the bubbling water jets and waterfall.

She stared at them, not moving, hoping one of them would look at her. Sue had her eyes closed and was also floating on her back. Tanya was staring off, apparently deep in thought.

Suddenly, the hand around her ankle pulled Ellen beneath the water. She kicked and flailed, her heart racing.

As she kicked against the invisible hand, she heard a woman's voice. It said, "Beware at the Biltmore. She knows you're coming."

Ellen choked out, "Who knows?"

The hand released her, and she struggled to her feet and stood up, coughing up water.

Sue also got to her feet. "You okay?"

"What happened?" Tanya asked.

Ellen couldn't speak. Shaking, she climbed from the tub and wrapped herself in a towel.

"Ellen?" Tanya asked.

"I need a minute," she said as she tried to gather her wits and calm her pounding heart.

CHAPTER FOUR

The Basilica of St. Lawrence

Ellen paid the cabbie outside of the Basilica of St. Lawrence in downtown Asheville before climbing out into the late morning sun beside Tanya and Sue. The red brick façade was three stories high with double wooden doors at the entrance and a tower on each end. The towers were several stories higher than the rest of the building and were each capped with a silver dome and cross. Behind the façade was the sanctuary with its enormous dome. Ellen had read about it in one of her Asheville books.

"Did you know that this church has the largest free-standing elliptical dome in North America?" she asked her friends. "And the architect, Rafael Guastavino, also built the domes in the Biltmore House."

"That's interesting," Tanya said.

"It's not that interesting," Sue said. "But thanks for sharing."

"What's interesting is the method," Ellen insisted. "He used layers of tiles tied together with mortar to create thin but strong arches. It was unique. That's why Vanderbilt wanted him. He was considered the best in the world."

"Hmm. Still not that interesting," Sue said.

"He also built the Smithsonian, the Metropolitan Museum of Art, and the vaulted arches at Central Station in New York."

"Well, I guess that's a little interesting," Sue admitted.

"He didn't use any wood beams or steel, and the roof is made of tile covered with copper."

"Okay, that's more than a little interesting," Sue said. "No wood at all?"

"None, making them fireproof."

"Impressive," Sue admitted.

As they made their way around the front toward the side entrance, they saw a little old man with a pair of clippers trimming a hedge. He was wearing faded, baggy jeans, a white long-sleeved shirt, and a straw hat.

"Good morning," he said to them.

Ellen thought he must be at least eighty-five and possibly older.

"Good morning," Ellen replied. "I know the doors don't open until eleven, but I was told we could come a little early."

"Are you the ghost hunters?" the man asked.

Recognizing his voice, Ellen said, "Yes. Are you Father Donovan?"

"Right you are. Come this way, and I'll let you inside."

"Thank you so much for this opportunity," Sue said.

"Yes, we really appreciate it," Tanya said. "Ellen read that it's the most haunted place in Asheville."

"Oh, I agree." Father Donovan fished his keys from his trouser pocket and unlocked the door. "I've personally felt the presence of many ghosts."

"Really?" Ellen asked as he opened the door for them. "Anything you'd care to share?"

"A fellow priest and good friend of mine died in the rectory, oh, about twenty years ago. It was sudden. He was watching television one night and dropped dead. He was loved by me and by all our parishioners. We don't think he ever left us."

"Why do you believe that, Father?" Sue asked.

"Well, you see, he wore a certain cologne—sometimes a little too much of it, if you ask me, and you can be in the church praying, or kneeling at the high altar, or perhaps walking down the aisle toward a pew, and you'll suddenly get a whiff of his cologne, even when no one else is around."

"How interesting," Ellen said.

"What was his name?" Tanya asked. "Maybe we can talk to him today."

"Jonathon Peters. If you do, tell him Will Donovan says hello and to lay off the cologne."

"Sure thing," Ellen said with a grin.

"Aren't you concerned as to why he hasn't moved on?" Sue asked. "Wouldn't he find peace in Heaven?"

The priest lifted a finger. "Heaven is a state of mind, not a place. I believe Father Peters is happy here. Some feel as though he continues to serve his parishioners by praying for them."

"So, you believe it's possible to be here and in Heaven at the same time?" Ellen asked.

"Indeed, I do. I believe some souls may move on to another dimension, if you will, but others find their Heaven here. God's heavenly kingdom is all around us. Some may even move back and forth between dimensions. It's more about how they find peace than where they find it, in my opinion, but it's only a matter of faith, you see. I suppose none of us knows until it's our time. Now, I need to get back to work. Do you have any other questions for me before I go?"

"How long do we have to conduct our investigation?" Sue asked.

"I hear confessions this evening beginning at four-thirty. You're welcome to stay till then."

"We'll be out of your hair before then, Father," Ellen said. "We have a wedding rehearsal and dinner to attend at the Biltmore tonight."

"Oh, how wonderful. I just love weddings."

"It's my son's," Ellen said. "I couldn't be happier for him."

"Nor I," Father Donovan said with a smile. "Well, I'll be right outside if you need anything. Good luck with your ghost hunting."

"Thank you, Father," Tanya said.

When the old priest left, Sue said, "It's too bad the parishioners don't hire someone to trim the hedges for him. I don't mean to say he's too old, but if he were milk, I'd sniff him."

"Maybe he enjoys doing it himself," Tanya put in.

"Maybe so. Now that you say that, it reminds me of the crew I hired recently to cut our lawn. It's a husband-and-wife team in their seventies. I didn't know they were that old when I hired them. They did our neighbors' lawn, and I liked how it looked, so I asked for their number."

"Did they do a good job?" Ellen asked.

"They did an excellent job," Sue said, "but I felt kind of bad. They were probably wondering why I wasn't out there doing it myself."

"I'm sure they were glad to do it," Ellen said. "And older gardeners know more than the young ones do. They do a better job. With age comes wisdom."

"And hairs growing in strange places that need to be plucked," Sue added.

"Not everyone enjoys yardwork," Tanya said. "Maybe they do. You shouldn't feel bad."

"Tom made me feel worse when he came home and asked why I'd hired the retirement home to take care of our yard. It really is a lot of work."

"Speaking of work," Ellen said as she pulled her full-spectrum camera from her shoulder bag. "Let's get busy. According to one of my Asheville books, the architect came here to work on the Biltmore and fell in love with Asheville, so he moved his family here."

"That seems to have happened a lot," Tanya pointed out.

"After Rafael joined this parish, he offered to build this church for free."

"That was generous," Sue said. "It must have been a pretty shabby place for him to want to redo it."

"Not necessarily," Tanya said.

"Anyway, he loved this church so much that he was buried here, inside the sanctuary, beneath the altar. People say he never left."

"So that's two," Tanya said. "The priest and the architect. Who were the others you mentioned?"

"The architect's wife and daughter," Ellen said. "Unlike Rafael, they were buried in the cemetery, but people have sworn over the years to have seen them."

"Really? They saw full-bodied apparitions?" Tanya asked.

"That's what one of my books said." Then Ellen added, "Rafael's wife was named Frances, and his daughter was . . . oh, I can't remember her name. Anyway, I also read that hundreds of spirit orbs have been captured on digital cameras over the years."

"Cool," Tanya said. "I hope we capture something."

"I'll take some initial temperature readings," Sue said as she pulled out her instrument. "Do you want to set up your camera?"

"I didn't bring a tripod, but I think this is a good place." Ellen turned on her camera and set it on the altar, pointed toward the pews.

"Where do you want this nimrod?" Tanya asked.

Ellen laughed. "REM-POD, you nimrod."

"You're hilarious," Tanya said. "I'll just put it here in the center aisle."

Ellen took out her phone and opened the ghost box app. "I'll just set this beside the camera, so it can pick up anything we might miss."

Once her equipment was in place, Ellen stepped down from the dais and sat in a pew five rows back, just behind Tanya and across from Sue.

For the first time, she looked around the sanctuary. Gorgeous stained glass windows depicting images from Jesus's life surrounded them. The walls were adorned with statues of saints. Above the high altar, which looked to be made of marble, was a crucifix carved in wood with the figures of Mary and probably an apostle mourning the death of Jesus. Behind the wood carving, and covering the entire wall, were ornamental partitions made of what appeared to be chrome and terra cotta tiles depicting six figures. Ellen wasn't sure if they were archangels or apostles or some of both.

The walls and floor were made of limestone tiles in a cream-colored hue—a nice contrast to the wooden pews and crucifixion scene. But the most breathtaking architectural feature was the dome ceiling, its intricate tilework magnificent in both its strength and beauty.

"Do you want to start?" Sue asked Ellen from where she sat across the aisle from her. "Or should I?"

"You go ahead," Ellen said.

They hadn't made a circle of protection because it wasn't necessary in this holy place. The holy water, incense, and constant petitions and prayers by priests and parishioners kept the sanctuary clean of negative energy.

They also hadn't lighted candles because the candelabras near the altar had already been lit.

"Spirits of the other realm," Sue began. "We come in peace. We mean no harm. We are hoping for the opportunity to speak with you. If there is anyone here who would like to communicate with us, please feel free to make yourself known. You can pull energy from the candlelight and the holy water. You can also feed from the electricity in our devices. We would love to see you or hear you, but if you can't manifest yourselves, we invite you to use the REM-POD located in the aisle. If you touch it, it will beep and shine a yellow light. Or you can use the phone on the altar beside our camera. If you hear that white noise, well, that's coming from the ghost box app. You can choose the words you want to convey from among several different radio frequencies and channels. So, having said all of that, is anyone here with us?"

Ellen glanced around the church, hoping for a sign. When several seconds passed in silence, she feared their coming had been a waste of their time.

"Is there anyone here who would like to speak with us?" Sue repeated. "We mean you no harm. We come in peace. We'd just like to chat with you today."

The REM-POD beeped and made Ellen flinch. She smiled with excitement and saw it mirrored in the faces of her friends.

"If you wish to speak with us," Sue began, "please touch the REM-POD twice. If you want us to leave, touch it once."

The REM-POD beeped once.

Ellen frowned and was about to speak when the REM-POD beeped a second time.

She lifted her chin and smiled at her friends. "They want us to stay."

"Who are we speaking with?" Sue asked. "Is this the architect, Rafael? If so, please make the REM-POD beep twice. If not, make it beep once."

The REM-POD did not go off for several seconds, but then a word came over the ghost app.

"Did you get that?" Ellen asked, not sure what she heard.

"I think it said Frances," Tanya said.

Just then, the ghost app said, "Yes . . . Frances."

"That's the architect's wife!" Ellen said as the three friends shared more excited smiles.

The ghost app said, "Yes . . . true."

"She's confirming that she's Rafael's wife," Tanya said.

"Thanks so much for speaking with us, Frances," Sue said. "By any chance, is Father Peterson with you?"

The ghost app said, "Not yet."

"Not yet," Tanya repeated.

"Does that mean you're expecting him later?" Ellen asked.

The ghost app said, "Confession."

"Oh!" Tanya said. "Maybe he's coming to hear her confession later today."

"But why would a ghost need to confess?" Sue wondered out loud.

"Yes," the ghost app said. "Rafael."

"Oh, my gosh!" Tanya cried. "She's referring to her husband."

"What about Rafael?" Ellen asked.

One of the candles near the altar went out, leaving a dark trail of smoke in place of the flame.

The ghost app said, "Yes . . . he is here."

"Raphael is here?" Sue asked.

"Yes," the ghost app said. "He was . . . at Biltmore House."

Ellen's mouth dropped open. "Did you say that Rafael was at Biltmore House?"

"Sometimes," the ghost app said.

"Sometimes Rafael visits Biltmore House?" Sue asked.

Another candle by the altar was extinguished.

"Yes . . . but . . . listen."

"We're listening," Sue said. "Is there something you want to tell us?"

"Yes . . . Please . . . watch out."

"Watch out? Watch out for what?" Ellen asked.

"She . . . is waiting . . . for you."

"Who is waiting for us?" Sue asked. "And where?"

"Biltmore."

Ellen's eyes widened as a chill crept down the back of her neck.

"Who's waiting for us at the Biltmore?" Sue asked.

They hoped for something other than the white noise to come over the ghost app on Ellen's phone, but several seconds went by, and then a full minute, before Sue said, "Frances? Are you still there?"

The REM-POD beeped twice.

"Maybe the name of the person waiting for us hasn't come up on any of the frequencies and channels," Tanya said.

The REM-POD beeped twice.

"Should we use the Ouija Board to get the name?" Ellen wondered.

"I don't think we should use it in a Catholic Church," Sue said. "We might open the door for evil to come in."

"Frances?" Ellen asked. "Will we be in danger at the Biltmore?"

The REM-POD beeped twice.

CHAPTER FIVE

The Rehearsal

I don't know why I'm nervous," Maya said from where she sat beside Lane and Ellen in the back of the Grove Park Inn shuttle. "It's just the rehearsal."

Ellen patted Maya's hand. Maya was dressed in a cream sweater and cream flared pants with taupe boots and wore a cream headband with little ivory rosebuds across it. She looked adorable beside Lane, who looked handsome in black slacks and a gray button-down shirt.

"Sometimes it's hard to tell the difference between being excited and being nervous," Ellen said. "I bet you're excited because there's truly nothing to be nervous about."

Ellen wished she could feel surer of her words, but after the warnings at both the spa and the basilica, she wasn't confident that there was nothing to be nervous about. Tanya and Sue had promised to help her to keep an eye out for whoever it was that was waiting for them at the Biltmore.

"You're right," Maya said with a smile.

Lane stroked Maya's chestnut hair. "Everything's going to be fine—more than fine."

Brian, who sat in the middle seat beside Sue and Tanya, reached back and squeezed Ellen's knee. "That was us not that long ago."

Ellen leaned forward and kissed his cheek.

"No making out in the shuttle," Sue teased. "It's not fair to those of us without our husbands."

"And if Tom were here, you'd be going at it," Tanya said sarcastically to Sue.

"That's right," Sue said. "And you'd be enjoying every minute of it. You might even take notes."

"So much for that yield sign," Ellen teased, forgetting that Ted and Gayle Stone were with them in the seat behind the driver.

"Well, I wouldn't be wearing it on my face," Sue shot back.

"Do I want to know what you're talking about?" Brian asked.

"I'll tell you later," Ellen said.

"But then she'll have to kill you," Sue said as she gave Ellen the evil eye.

The sun was beginning to set, making the sparkling Christmas lights surrounding the Biltmore that much more spectacular—especially those on an enormous Christmas tree covered in white lights on the front lawn near a large fountain. The ceremony would take place about fifty yards from the fountain near the Biltmore House.

The house was built out of white limestone and was adorned with terraces, gables, spires, and towers. The gray-tiled roof added a stark contrast to the limestone that seemed to glisten in the setting sun like the distant mountains. Even the mountains were dwarfed by the castle that towered over the landscape.

On the front lawn of the house, a dozen rows of white wooden chairs had been set up with a white carpeted aisle running up the middle toward a grapevine arch covered in white roses and tulle. More white roses and tulle adorned a black iron gate that decorated the back entrance to the area.

"Oh, it's so beautiful," Maya said.

"Are you crying?" Lane asked. "Aww. You're so cute."

"No," she said, unconvincingly. "I'm just blown away."

"It's truly magical," Ellen said, feeling pleased that her son and his bride would have a fairytale wedding—a wonderful start to what she hoped would be a wonderful life together.

"Look," Lane said. "That's Christian and Teresa."

"Isn't that Curtis and Jeffrey with them?" Maya asked.

"Oh, you're right."

The shuttle stopped and let the party out into the chilly evening, and they met up with those who were waiting to rehearse the ceremony.

Ellen enjoyed watching her son embrace his best friends—Jeffrey, Curtis, and Christian—friends since elementary school. Ellen was happy that Maya had become close to them, too. They attended concerts and art shows together and got together for video gaming at least once a month. Christian was the only friend who was married. He'd married his high school sweetheart, Teresa, who was also in the wedding as one of Maya's bridesmaids.

Wishing Alison and Nolan had been able to make it this evening for the rehearsal, Ellen went around greeting the others with hugs and handshakes. She met Maya's maid of honor and best friend from college, Jen, and Maya's little sister, Sammy, who was a junior bridesmaid. Although she'd met Maya's parents via Zoom, this was the first time they were meeting in person.

Greg and Karen Stone were young and beautiful, making Ellen feel a little old and dowdy. Karen was petite with short, chestnut hair, the same color as Maya's. Greg was tall, like his father. His dark blond hair was short and combed back. To Ellen, he resembled a young Nicholas Cage.

Those that weren't needed for the rehearsal were escorted to the Stable Loft, where dinner was to be served. Sue and Tanya followed Ted and Gayle, giving Ellen and Brian a wave goodbye.

The wedding coordinator, a thin woman in her mid-thirties named Patricia, positioned everyone else in their places while making introductions where needed. The minister, a young man with a friendly smile, waited patiently for the rehearsal to begin.

Lane was instructed to escort Maya's parents down the aisle first. Then he returned for Ellen and Brian. Ellen giggled beside her son as he joked about the possibility of a blizzard the day of the wedding.

"It's fifty degrees," she pointed out. "And it's supposed to be the same tomorrow."

"I know," he said, his blue eyes gleaming. "I just wanted to make you laugh."

She kissed his cheek and sat on the front row on the groom's side.

The bridesmaids followed, beginning with the junior bridesmaid, Sammy. Alison and Nolan would have to be caught up to speed later tonight.

"They would be here by now if you had let them fly in my jet," Brian said, reading her mind.

Ellen chuckled. "You know me better than that."

After she, Sue, and Tanya had endured a crash landing in his jet during their case at the Hoover Dam, she could rarely be persuaded to fly in it or allow her children to do so, either.

"True," he said.

As she watched Maya walk down the aisle with her father toward Lane and the minister, Ellen's eyes watered. She couldn't believe her baby boy was getting married. She was both happy and sad.

She was sad that time had flown by so quickly and sad that Paul couldn't be here to see their second son become a husband. She wondered if Paul was watching from above, and, if so, if he was bothered by the fact that Brian was sitting beside her with his arm draped across her shoulder, keeping her warm.

After the rehearsal, the wedding party strolled across the lawn toward the Biltmore House as the last of the tourists were catching the shuttles and leaving the property. Approaching the house, Ellen noticed the dozens of gargoyles near the terraces, gables, and spires. Each one was unique. She spotted a horned monster, a fat accordion player, a beggar, a monk, a lioness with human breasts, a devil, and a mandolin player.

To the right of the house, they walked through a carriage porch and a stable courtyard, where food shops were closing, to the stables, which had been renovated into a shopping center and restaurant and, tonight, had been transformed into a winter wonderland of lights, tulle, and white roses. Wooden cathedral ceilings sparkled as they reflected the lights. Two round tables and one long rectangular one were decorated with gorgeous glass vases filled with white rosebuds.

The other guests were already seated. Ellen had made sure that Sue and Tanya would be at the same table with her and Brian. According to the name cards, Maya's other set of grandparents—James and Melissa Dresden—would be seated there as well. Ellen noticed that Maya and Lane sat at the other round table with Maya's parents and Ted and Gayle Stone on the opposite side of the room. Between them sat the rest of the wedding party at the long rectangular table, including the minister, who now stood up and led them in prayer before the servers began bringing in delectable plates of turkey, dressing, gravy, mashed potatoes, asparagus, and buttery rolls.

As the plates were being brought to the table, an older couple joined them and introduced themselves as James and Melissa Dresden, Maya's grandparents.

"Sorry we're late," Melissa said as James pulled out her chair for her and she took her seat.

"It's so nice to meet you," Ellen said to Maya's Vanderbilt relatives. "I'm Lane's mother, Ellen, and this is my husband, Brian. These are my friends, Tanya and Sue."

"Nice to meet you," Melissa said.

The Dresdens were short and stout—James with red hair peppered with gray and Melissa with short, chestnut hair cut in a bob. Melissa's hair was thick and lustrous, reminding Ellen of both Maya and Karen's.

Like the rival set of grandparents, they appeared to be in their late six-ties.

"It's an honor," Sue, still an inch shorter than they, added with too much enthusiasm. "We're grateful for the chance to see this magnificent place."

"You're the ghost busters, aren't you?" James said. "Maya told us about you."

Ellen smiled. "Yes, that's right—though we're more healers than busters. We try to bring peace to tethered spirits."

"We have a ghost in our house," Melissa said. "I think it's an old man. He keeps moving things around."

James waved a hand through the air. "She loses things and doesn't want the blame. There's no ghost—not one I've ever seen."

"Just because you've never seen it doesn't mean it isn't there," Ellen said. It was the same thing Tanya had told Ellen several years ago, be-fore Ellen had begun to believe.

James said nothing in reply. Melissa smiled at Ellen, and Ellen real-ized in that moment that she'd made a friend.

Ellen had just finished her dinner when dessert was served—cheesecake topped with cherries and flecks of chocolate. Greg Stone, the father of the bride, stood up to make a toast.

Reminding Ellen again of Nicholas Cage, Greg said, "I just want to thank everyone for coming tonight, and I'd like to say a few words. When Maya first told us about Lane, we were worried, because she'd never been in a serious relationship before, and she's our first born, so we were inexperienced. Karen immediately went on the Internet to find out everything she could learn about him."

"Uh-oh," Lane said with a wink at Maya.

The room filled with laughter.

"Fortunately, she discovered that Lane was a UT graduate and a tal-ented artist and musician with a great future ahead of him. He came from a good family and had a lot of friends who cared about him. Then, when Maya brought him to Asheville to meet us, we knew he was the one for her. We'd never seen her happier, which made us happy, too."

Greg lifted his glass. "Please raise your glasses and join me in toasting to the bride and groom."

"To the bride and groom!" everyone said as their glasses clinked together.

After Ellen took a sip of wine, she stood up to make a toast, too.

Her heart raced in her chest as she glanced around the room. Her heart rejoiced for Lane and grieved for Paul, who should have been here at their son's wedding. But she was grateful for her life with Brian and so pleased that her best friends could be here during this important time in her life.

"Thank you all so much for being here," she said as she fought tears. "Each of you is important to this new family that is about to be formed between these two lovely young people—my son, Lane, and his beautiful bride, Maya. I admit I was surprised when they announced their engagement. They're so young. But they've been dating for nearly a year and, as Greg said, they exude love and happiness wherever they go. Their love for one another has filled my heart with joy. If Lane's father, Paul, were here he'd be so proud." Ellen lifted her glass and said, "To the bride and groom."

"To the bride and groom!" the others said as they clinked their glasses together once more.

Ellen felt wary when Maya's grandfather, James, who sat across the table from her, stood up with his glass.

"I'd like to toast the couple, too. Lane and Maya, life can be hard. It can be amazing, but it can be devastating, too. Lane knows, because he lost his father. Maya, I don't think you've known that kind of loss yet. Trust me. I've lived a long time. Hell, if someone told me to act my age, I'd probably drop dead."

James paused for a moment while everyone laughed at his joke.

"Two heads are better than one," he continued. "When you have someone to lean on, it makes the hard times in life easier to get through. That's the promise you're about to make to each other tomorrow. You're promising to be there for each other, to help one another through the hard times." He lifted his glass in the air. "Here's hoping you both show up tomorrow, so no one's stranded at the altar."

The crowd laughed again.

"To the bride and groom!" several people said as more glasses clinked.

Then Maya's other grandfather, Ted Stone, stood up, looking like an angry Mr. Clean. "Of course they're going to show up tomorrow, James. Why would you say something like that? Is that a jab at me? I should have known you couldn't speak without taking a jab at me."

"No one's jabbing anyone, Dad," Greg said.

"If the shoe fits," James said.

Ellen covered her mouth, feeling helpless to stop the scene from unfolding before her.

"Really, James?" Melissa chastised. "Did you have to say that?"

"Let me make my toast," Ted demanded. "If the good die young, James Dresden is going to live a very long time."

"That's not funny coming from you," James snarled.

"Okay, okay," Ted said, waving his hand through the air. "Seriously, though, James is right about one thing. Life is hard. So, when you choose to spend it with someone, make sure it's the right one. Make sure it's for the right reason. Marriage can last a long time. I mean, you hope it lasts forever, and you don't want to be with someone who doesn't truly love you. There has to be chemistry. And I can see by the way you two are looking at one another that you have it. Cheers to the bride and groom."

"To the bride and groom!" the crowd said.

Across the table from Ellen, Melissa's face was red, and tears had welled in her eyes.

"Let's get out of here," James said to her. "Let's get you home."

"No, it's fine, James," Melissa said.

"It is not fine." James stood up. "Some people will always be ass-holes. Come on. Let's go."

Melissa looked mortified. She jumped to her feet and fled the room with her husband ambling behind her. Maya noticed and tried to intercept. James hugged her, whispered something in her ear, and followed Melissa out.

"What the heck?" Sue asked Ellen.

Ellen shook her head. "This is not a good sign."

"I wonder what happened between them," Tanya said, before taking a sip of her wine.

The server who was clearing their plates bent close to Ellen. "If you want to know their story, come see me at my shop tomorrow morning."

Ellen looked up at her. "Excuse me?"

The woman reached into her trouser pocket and pulled out a card. She handed it to Ellen.

It read: *Shiri Walker, Instant Karma, 36 N. Lexington Ave., Asheville, NC.*

Before Ellen could ask the server more about it, the woman left with her arms full of dirty dishes.

CHAPTER SIX

Instant Karma

While Sue rode with Maya, Lane, and a few others back to the Grove Park Inn after the rehearsal dinner, Ellen, Brian, and Tanya took a different shuttle to the airport to meet their kids. Just as they suspected, Ellen's kids flew in on the same plane as Tanya's.

Bri was fast asleep in Taylor's arms, and she and Nolan looked exhausted. Taylor's blonde hair was uncombed, and her blue eyes were rimmed with smudged makeup. Nolan's dark, wavy hair was also a mess, and his green eyes had dark crescent moons beneath them.

"Now she decides to sleep," Nolan said of Bri as he hugged Ellen hello. "She wouldn't sit still on the plane."

"We're so ready for bed," Taylor said as she offered hugs, too.

"Hi, Mom," Alison said. Alison's dark brown hair fell to her shoulders, and her hazel eyes gleamed. She was the only one in the group who appeared rested.

Ellen hugged and kissed them each on the cheek. Then she hugged Cammie, Mike, and Seth—Tanya's daughter, son, and son-in-law.

During the ride to the hotel, Ellen, Brian, and Tanya described the rehearsal and the dinner to the new arrivals, including the disagreement between the two sets of grandparents. But, not wanting to sound like a gossip, Ellen didn't mention the shop owner who'd given Ellen her card.

It wasn't until the next day, during the bridal brunch on the Sunset Terrace, that Ellen, who was holding her sweet granddaughter on her lap, mentioned the Instant Karma shop owner to Sue and Tanya.

"She said she would tell me what happened so long ago between the grandparents," Ellen whispered, not wanting to be overheard by Maya's mother and Gayle Stone, seated with Maya at another table.

Ellen had noticed that Melissa Dresden was conspicuously absent, but maybe she hadn't been invited.

Tanya took a sip of her hot tea. "Do you think she really knows?"

Sue leaned on her elbows. "Why would she say she did if she didn't? What would be her motive for lying?"

"I don't know," Tanya said. "Attention? Maybe she just wants us to shop at her store."

"That doesn't make sense," Sue said. "We may as well check it out. Don't you think, Ellen?"

"I suppose it wouldn't hurt to go and see what she has to say," Ellen admitted. "I think I'd regret it if we didn't, because I'd be thinking about it, you know?"

Just then, Gayle Stone lifted her mimosa and said, "Now some advice for the bride. They say you should never go to bed angry." Then, in a mocking tone, she added, "I guess that means it's better to stay up all night fighting."

Ellen laughed along with the others.

"It's also important to note," Gayle continued, "that marriage is a relationship in which one person is always right and the other is the husband."

"Oh, I like her," Tanya said before taking a sip of her hot tea.

"Also, listening to your husband might sometimes feel like reading the terms and conditions on a website," Gayle said. "You won't always understand, but it's best to say *I agree*."

Sue guffawed. Then, with her voice lowered, she added, "The chopped liver is looking better and better by the minute."

"And last, but not least," Gayle said. "Always remember that marriage is about falling in love many times, but always with the same person. Cheers."

The other ladies raised their glasses and said in unison, "Cheers."

"Nana, look," Bri said, pointing.

Ellen followed her granddaughter's little finger to a dog—a service animal. He was a small black lab sitting at the feet of Maya's little sister, Sammy.

"You see the puppy?" Ellen said in a soft voice. "He's a cutie, isn't he?"

"I want puppy," Bri said.

"Oh, sweet baby girl. Your parents already have their hands full."

Tanya and Sue laughed.

It was approaching noon when Ellen and her friends were in a cab on their way to Lexington Avenue. Their driver was a young woman with a nose ring and a tattoo of a flower on the side of her neck.

"Merry Christmas eve," the driver greeted them as they'd strapped themselves in.

"Merry Christmas eve," they replied.

"Are you shopping for anything in particular at Instant Karma?" she asked.

"Not really," Sue said from beside Ellen.

Tanya, who sat in front, asked, "Are you familiar with the store?"

"Oh, yeah. I love it. I buy all my crystals there. I just bought this rose quartz there last week." She flashed them a view of her hand. Her fingers were adorned with rings. "They have good, quality stones."

"That's good to know," Ellen said.

"Shiri also does readings. Did you know that? She's really good. She makes the best potions, too. She made me a love potion last month and now I'm in love with the nicest guy."

"Wasn't the potion to get him to fall in love with you?" Sue wondered.

The cabbie laughed. "You would think, but honestly, guys fall for me all the time. I'm the one who can't seem to connect."

The driver pulled up to the curb in front of Instant Karma, a little shop with a colorful mandala in the front window.

"We're here," she said. "Tell Shiri that Dawn says hi."

"Will do," Ellen said as she paid the driver. "Would you mind waiting for us? We won't be long."

"No problem."

"Thanks," Ellen said as she climbed from the cab.

Tanya opened the shop door for Sue and Ellen.

"Thank you very much," Ellen said as she entered the whimsical space. It smelled of incense and oregano.

Rows of displays with various sizes of raw gemstones took up the center of the room. Along the walls were decks of tarot cards, jars of potions, and tiny bags of dried herbs, reminding Ellen of the *gris gris* she wore around her neck. The glass counter displayed rings, pendants, bracelets, and earrings with various stones embedded in them.

"You came," the woman from behind the counter said. Shiri Walker was as tall and thin as Tanya. She was darker complected and wore her black, kinky hair tied at the nape of her neck with a colorful scarf. Her denim dress was loose-fitting, as were the bangles on each of her long, thin arms.

Sue shrugged. "You made it hard not to."

"Dawn says hi," Ellen said, as promised.

"Oh, she's one of my best customers."

"Do you really know why the Dresdens don't get along with the Stones?" Tanya asked.

"Yes. Not many know," she said. "But I do."

"Why did you offer to tell me their story?" Ellen asked with her eyes narrowed.

"I could read your positive energy," she said. "And there are two ghosts at Biltmore who want your help."

Ellen exchanged looks of bewilderment with her friends. "What makes you say that?"

"I've been able to see ghosts since I was a little girl. They talk to me. Last night, two of them came to me. One, whom I've never met before, approached me outside in the courtyard. Apparently, she couldn't get your attention."

"Who is she?" Sue asked.

"She didn't say, but she had a lot of negative energy around her. I'd be careful if I were you. I'm not sure if she can be trusted."

"I wonder why she wants to talk to *us*?" Sue said. "Why wouldn't she just tell *you* whatever it is she needs to say?"

"I have no idea," Shiri said.

"And the other one?" Ellen asked.

"She's been talking to me for a long time," Shiri said. "I used to work at Biltmore House full-time before I opened my shop five years ago. I still work there part-time in the evenings during events, and the spirit visits me regularly."

"What's her name?" Ellen asked.

"Melinda Brown. She claims to be a sister to Melissa Brown—now Melissa Dresden."

Ellen lifted her brows.

"What did she tell you?" Sue wanted to know.

"She said that Melissa was originally engaged to Ted Stone, but Melissa didn't want to marry Ted."

"So, it wasn't Melissa who was stood up at the altar?" Tanya asked. "It was Ted?"

"No. It was Melissa," Shiri explained, "but she asked Ted not to show up. Melinda didn't learn this truth until after she died."

Ellen gasped. "Why in the world would any bride do that to herself?"

"Her parents would have disowned her if she had broken off the engagement," Shiri said. "At least, that's what the ghost told me. So, Melissa begged Ted not to show up and to take the fall for her, and, because he loved her, he did."

"Wow," Tanya said. "Clearly her husband, James, doesn't know the truth. I wonder why."

"Only Ted and Melissa seem to know," Shiri said. "But the ghost wants you to convince Melissa to tell the truth to the family. She says it's the only way she—the ghost—can find peace."

"I wonder why Melissa's ordeal impacts the sister," Tanya said.

"I think there's something Melinda isn't telling me," Shiri admitted.

Ellen scratched her chin. "I'm not sure how we can interfere without ruffling a lot of feathers."

"I guess we could start by reaching out to the ghost," Sue said. "Maybe she can tell us what to do."

"Lane's wedding has to come first," Ellen said. "Promise me that."

"Of course," Tanya said.

"We promise," Sue agreed.

"Would you have time to do a reading?" Tanya asked. "Maybe you could shed some light on what's waiting for as at the Biltmore."

"I'd be happy to," Shiri said. "I usually charge fifty dollars, but I'll do yours for free, since I asked you to come."

"No, we're happy to pay for your time," Sue said.

Shiri reached into a drawer and pulled out a deck, which she immediately began to shuffle.

"Do you want to ask a specific question?" Shiri asked.

Ellen sucked in her lips. "Hmm. Yes. How can we help the spirits at the Biltmore?"

Shiri held out the deck. "Cut?"

Ellen cut the deck and returned it to Shiri, who then laid out six cards, the first of which was an angel with two cups. It was called *Temperance.*

"This first card represents where you are now in the big picture. See how the angel is mixing substances in the two cups? The card suggests that your soul is going through a similar process of being remade. This phase you're entering will break you and make you new."

Ellen wasn't sure she liked the sound of that.

"This second card shows your current place in the bigger picture."

The card was a ram-headed creature called *The Devil*.

"Oh, dear," Sue said.

"It's not bad," Shiri said. "It just represents the realm of the taboo— the wild side of us that society has demonized. This card demonstrates that you will be empowered to overcome prejudicial stereotypes to experience real freedom."

"It's talking about the Ouija Board, I bet," Tanya said. "Some people turn their noses up at people who attempt to use it, even for good."

"That, or any involvement with the occult," Shiri said. "Most people don't know it or don't talk about it, but Paganism was demonized by early Christians to encourage people to convert. Pagans worship natural deities later depicted by Christians as demons. Even today, pagans are stigmatized, and their beliefs aren't viewed as religious but as demonic."

"I didn't know that," Ellen said.

"Anyway, this third card represents your heart's desire. It's *The Tower*. As you can see, it's on fire, and figures are falling from it. It suggests that you desire to topple the hierarchy and to liberate oppressed people through social change."

"That's exactly what we're trying to do," Tanya said with wide eyes. "We're trying to free spirits from the chains that bind them, and often those chains are forged by people."

"Well said, Tanya," Ellen said. "What's this fourth card mean?"

It was called *The Star*, and it featured a naked woman pouring a vessel of water into a small pool while one large star and many smaller stars shone overhead.

"This placement represents the lesson to be learned," Shiri said. "The Star reminds you that you are an agent of the divine and that, if you listen to the universe, you will feel it nudging you toward a destiny."

Sue folded her arms across her chest. "That's spot on. That's the lesson we all need to learn, don't you think, Ellen?"

"Yes. I thought I already knew that lesson, though. Sounds like I'm about to relearn it."

Shiri pointed to the fifth card. "This card represents the freedom you will gain when you learn that lesson."

The card was called *The Moon*, and it depicted a moon face looking down on earth, where a wolf, coyote, and crab were harking to it from below.

"The Moon represents a state of transcended consciousness in which the membrane between the individual and the unknown disappears, and you receive visions, insights, and deep mystical realities beyond what your ordinary senses can provide. You essentially become a shaman."

A chill snaked down Ellen's back. "It's what we want, isn't it? To communicate with the dead, to try to help, right?"

"Right," Sue said. "But it sounds scarier when Shiri describes it. I'm not sure I want that membrane between us and the unknown to leave us completely. Can't we just have a peek without seeing the whole show?"

Ellen and Shiri laughed. Tanya looked as white as a Garbanzo bean.

Shiri shrugged. "If you're called, you're called. Agent of the divine, remember?"

"Oh, boy," Ellen said before she sucked in her lips. "Okay, so what's the final card?"

"That represents your new beginning."

The card was called *The Sun*, and it showed a sun face above a field of sunflowers and a naked child riding a white horse.

"What's it mean?" Ellen asked.

"Under the light of the sun, you become your authentic self, filled with primordial goodness and beauty. You are no longer shackled by the demonizing forces of society but are truly free and one with the divine. It's basically saying that you can do no wrong."

"That sounds optimistic," Sue said. "I like that one better than the Moon. It sounds less frightening."

Shiri tilted her head to the side. "I rarely see a spread consisting of all major arcana."

"What does that even mean?" Ellen asked. "I know very little about tarot."

"Well, the major arcana are the most powerful cards in the deck. The others are known as minor arcana. They consist of suits—like cups, pentacles, and wands. When the *minor* arcana appear in the spread, they suggest that you can change things, and they point to how. But when the *major* arcana appear in the spread, the universe is in control, and there's little you can do about it. A full spread of major arcana indicates that something huge is about to happen, and that's why you need to give over your will to the divine. The universe is about to use you to make something powerful happen."

"I'm not sure how I feel about that," Ellen said, feeling weak in the knees. "That's a lot to take in."

"It seems you don't have a choice," Shiri said. "So, regarding your initial question, I would interpret this spread to mean that you must allow the universe to work through you."

"That doesn't tell me a whole lot," Ellen said with a sigh.

"I think the answers you seek will be revealed to you in due time," Shiri said. "You've clearly been chosen. It's up to you to accept the mantle."

Ellen turned to her friends. "We accept, don't we, ladies?"

"I suppose we do," Tanya said.

"Whatever that entails," Sue added with her brows raised.

"You might want to consider arming yourselves," Shiri suggested. "Do you wear anything for protection?"

Sue chuckled. "I haven't had a period in six years."

Shiri blushed, "No, I meant…"

"Sue knows what you meant." Ellen showed her the *gris gris* she wore on a thin cord around her neck, tucked beneath her blouse. "This was made by a Voodoo high priestess in New Orleans."

"Do you know what herbs are in there?" Shiri asked. "Probably white sage, among other things."

"We have no clue," Tanya said.

"You might think about getting a black tourmaline ring or pendant. I have some here if you'd care to look. I'm not trying to pressure you into buying anything, though."

"That reminds me." Ellen dug in her purse for her wallet and brought out a fifty-dollar bill. "For the tarot reading."

"Thanks."

"Look at this ring," Tanya pointed out. "It's gorgeous and only twenty dollars. Is that black tourmaline?"

"It is. It's energy grounds you and blocks psychic attacks."

"Oooh. I think I'll get it. Can I try it on?"

Sue and Ellen also tried on rings, and they each bought one.

"Let's hope these help," Ellen said before they said goodbye to Shiri.

"Best of luck, ladies," Shiri said, waving. "I'll be there serving tonight if you need my help."

"We might just take you up on that," Sue said as they headed for the door.

CHAPTER SEVEN

Inside Biltmore House

Biltmore House was teeming with tourists at one o'clock in the afternoon when three shuttles from Grove Park Inn arrived with Ellen and a dozen other wedding guests, including the wedding party and Sue and Tanya and their families. No one was dressed yet for the wedding because they'd been promised a tour of the estate and gardens with plenty of time to get ready for the ceremony in their private rooms.

After they exited the shuttle, they pulled their luggage behind them toward the building's façade, where two lion statues guarded the entrance. Ellen, with Bri on her hip, saw her brother, Jody, his wife, June, and their sons, Trent and Trevor, aged five and six, waiting with their bags alongside some of the other guests.

"Jody!" Ellen waved.

It was so good to see him. They hadn't celebrated together last Christmas because Ellen and her family had spent it in Montana, and they'd missed each other at Thanksgiving because it was June's family's turn to host them. Ellen had intended to visit her brother in Kentucky over the summer, but it hadn't worked out.

"I'm so glad you could all make it," she said as she mussed Trent's hair and pinched Trevor's cheek.

"Is this Brianna?" Jody asked.

"It is. We call her Bri. Can you say hi to your Uncle Jody and Aunt June?"

"Hi," Bri said, with a finger in her mouth.

Just then, Paul's brother, Gordon, and his wife, Lou Cinda, caught up with them.

"You made it!" Lane said, giving them each a hug.

"Merry Christmas eve!" Ellen said.

"Merry Christmas eve," Lou Cinda replied. "This place is incredible."

Brian left Ellen's side to retrieve his brother and sister-in-law from the carriage porch.

They'd barely had time to finish their greetings when the wedding coordinator herded them from the front of the house to the library terrace on the far left of the building. The terrace was covered with an arbor made of dead vines entwined with holiday garlands and tiny white lights. All in all, there were forty-seven guests, including the minister, who were huddled there beneath the arbor excited about staying overnight at America's last castle, something that hadn't been done in decades.

While the wedding coordinator was giving her instructions to the group on the library terrace, Sue leaned toward Ellen and whispered, "I feel like I'm inside the gates of Willy Wonka's chocolate factory."

"That's the perfect analogy," Ellen whispered back. "I feel giddy."

The wedding coordinator, Patricia, handed out pamphlets while saying, "These maps of the second and third floor contain your room assignments along with luggage tags to attach to your bags, which will be safely secured in a storage room on the main floor until the house closes to the public at four o'clock. After that, they will be placed in your rooms for you. Tomorrow morning, your bags will be returned to this room until after your champagne breakfast and tour of the winery. They will then be delivered to the winery so you can pick them up before you leave Biltmore."

Ellen looked over her map. She and Brian had been assigned to the Louis XV room on the second floor. She couldn't wait to see it.

They were led from the terrace through a private outdoor gate at the back of the house and across a long porch, called the loggia, that over-looked the Blue Ridge Mountains. Tourists were taking photos and listening to hand-held audio tours as the wedding guests moved against the flow of traffic. Once inside, they passed an atrium called the winter garden, which was filled with deep red poinsettias and trimmed with ribboned garlands, a breakfast room that was larger than Ellen's dining room, and a huge butler's pantry before stopping outside of a storage room.

"Please tag your luggage and leave it here," Patricia said. "Then we'll break up into two groups and begin your tour of the house. We should finish by three, at which time you're invited to stroll through the gardens or grab a snack in the courtyard. At four o'clock, when the house closes to the public, you should find your rooms and begin dressing for to-night's ceremony. Everyone in the wedding party needs to be on the front lawn by five-thirty, so we can start on time at six."

"Are you ready to tour the castle?" Ellen asked Bri as she bounced her on her hip.

Bri nodded. "King and queen's castle?"

"You're the queen, Bri," she said. "How do you like that?"

Her grandbaby beamed.

The wedding coordinator broke them into two groups—a groom's group and a bride's group. The first was comprised of Lane's family and friends and the second of Maya's. However, Maya intervened and asked Ted and Gayle Stone to join the groom's group, to keep the feuding grandparents separated.

"You stick with Lane and me and the groom's group," she said to them with a smile.

"Why aren't you in the bride's group?" Maya's mother wanted to know.

Maya laced her fingers through Lane's. "Because we're inseparable."

Ellen shared a smile with Brian. She was so happy to see Lane happy.

The bride's group was led to the front of the house by one docent while another docent, a woman in her seventies named Linda, began the tour for the groom's group in the winter garden.

The round glass ceiling of the winter garden allowed the sun to shine over the circle of palms and other tropical plants along the perimeter of the room. At the center was a birdbath containing a statue of a boy holding a goose. It was planted with red poinsettias and bordered with pots of more poinsettias on the tiled floor. Above, ribboned garlands draped around eight hanging lanterns, forming an elegant inner ring in the circular, sunken room. Unlike the other rooms, the winter garden was not roped off and guests were allowed to walk freely inside.

"Wouldn't it be nice to have an indoor garden?" Tanya said from where she stood behind Ellen. "I'd grow herbs and make my own tea."

"But who'd take care of it when we're traveling?" Sue asked. "Dave?"

Dave scoffed. "Yeah, right."

Their conversation came to an end when Linda said, "It took six years for George Vanderbilt to build this 250-room home, and it took a community of craftsmen and the nation's best architects to make it happen. The first guests of the family were received in 1895. It was opened to the public in March of 1930. And the house continues to be family-owned and cared for by curators, conservators, and craftsmen."

The docent led them up a few steps from the sunken winter garden through a corridor to a billiard room at the front of the house.

"Now this is my kind of room," Dave said from behind the rope at the front of the group.

A fire flickered beneath a mantel decorated with Christmas garlands and fruit. Wood paneling, an intricate coffered ceiling, and wooden floors draped with Persian rugs gave the room a masculine feel while the Christmas tree near the fireplace filled it with holiday spirit.

"You could always turn one of the kids' bedrooms into a game room," Sue pointed out to Dave.

"One's a guest room and the other is my craft room," Tanya said. "He'd have to use the garage."

"But that's where I keep my Porsche," Dave said.

"Maybe you need a new house," Ellen said with a chuckle.

"We've honestly thought about it," Tanya admitted.

"Just past the billiard table to the right of that Christmas tree is a secret passage leading to a smoking room, a gun room, and a bachelors wing," Linda explained.

Dave lifted his brows to Tanya. "I want a smoking room."

"And I want a gun room," Sue said with a grin.

Lexi, Sue's married daughter, shook her head. "Oh, Mom."

From the billiard room, Linda led them to the banquet hall. "This is where you will feast tonight. The wooden barrel ceiling reaches seventy feet high, and this table seats thirty-eight. Two more additional tables will be brought in for tonight's dinner. While you're enjoying your meal later, remember that some of the world's most celebrated dignitaries have dined here as well."

The long wooden table had Christmas garlands and small Christmas trees running down its center, and the ornate chairs around it were upholstered in burgundy fabric. The same fabric hung in drapes around the arched entryways into the room.

Lane whispered near Ellen's ear, "I still can't believe I'm getting married here."

"Me neither," she said with a smile.

"How tall is that Christmas tree?" Maya asked of the tree towering above them on one side of the room.

"Thirty-seven feet," Linda said. "And it is illuminated with five hundred lights. Each year, we have a tree-raising ceremony that's quite an event."

"Wow," Maya said.

"The house is 175,000 square feet with thirty-three bedrooms, sixty-five fireplaces, forty-three bathrooms, and three kitchens, so it needed a banquet hall to match," Linda said with a smile.

The copper pipes of an organ were mounted on the wall above the Christmas tree, and the wall opposite had a white limestone triple fireplace with a fire blazing in each hearth. According to Linda, the walls were adorned with Flemish tapestries from the 1500s and crowned with mounted deer and antelope heads from the early 1900s.

Linda led them from the banquet hall back to the breakfast room where an oval table was set for ten. The table was covered with white lace linens, and the damask chairs were in the same burgundy color as the chairs in the banquet hall. The fireplace was decorated with more Christmas garlands. Tucked in the garlands were bright white ornaments like those that adorned the Christmas tree next to it. The ornate, gold coffered ceiling contrasted with the dark wooden floors.

"I'd like to draw your attention to the original art by Pierre-Auguste Renoir and John Singer Sargent," Linda said.

Ellen examined the Renoir more closely, and it took her breath away.

"Your paintings are better," Sue murmured beside her.

"You must want something," Ellen teased.

From the breakfast room, they entered a salon decorated in blues. A Christmas tree donning bright blue ornaments and ribbons of gold took center stage. Wooden chairs and benches were upholstered with floral embroidered fabric in the same blues and golds. These colors were also repeated in the large rug beneath the furniture arrangement. The ceiling, however, was covered with a billowy fabric treatment of deep burgundy and gold.

"Those chairs don't look very comfortable," Sue said.

"Maybe they didn't want their visitors to get too comfortable," Brian said with a laugh.

The breakfast room led to an oval-shaped music room. Brightly lit garlands draped over a unique fireplace that was made of limestone.

Above the mantle was the carving of a castle that resembled Biltmore House. Near the center of the room was a piano, and along three of the walls were built-in wooden shelves holding a sizeable library. Three floor to ceiling arched windows were draped with blue sheer curtains, and above them, the dark coffered ceiling of horizontal lines offered a contrast to the curved lines in the windows and furniture.

"You should play something for us," Maya whispered to Lane. "Maybe tonight, when the house is ours."

"I'm not sure we'll have access to this room," Ellen said.

"My mom said we do," Maya said. "She said we have we have access to everything in the south wing on the main floor and the basement."

Nolan raised his brows. "Oh, really? How cool."

"I'm beginning to feel like royalty," Tanya said.

"It really is amazing," Marcia, Brian's sister-in-law, said from the back of the group.

From the breakfast room, they walked through the front main hall with its white marble floors and dark coffered ceiling to a gallery room where three floor to ceiling tapestries, three brightly lit Christmas trees, and two limestone fireplaces with painted murals on them appeared on the main wall. Blue upholstered furniture was arranged into four different seating areas. The opposite side of the room had enormous arched windows with views of the loggia and the mountains beyond it.

"That's where we came in, right?" Brian said, pointing to the door to the outside loggia.

"Yes, I think so," Ellen said as Bri began to squirm in her arms.

"Mama," Bri said.

"I think she wants you," Ellen said to Taylor, who then stretched out her arms to receive her baby girl.

"Over here is a painting of Edith Vanderbilt," Linda said as she led them across the room. "She was the real heart of Biltmore House."

"That's what *I* said," Ellen whispered to Sue.

The gallery led to the most beautiful room Ellen had seen thus far: the library. The ceiling was open to two-stories with a balcony running all the way around the upper level. A spiral staircase at the far corner of the room, adjacent to the massive, black marble fireplace and walnut mantle, provided access to the second floor of books. Wooden chairs and couches cushioned with burgundy damask were positioned throughout the room on wooden floors. Matching drapes framed the two windows that overlooked the terrace, where the wedding coordinator had first gathered the guests before entering the house.

But the most impressive element in the library, aside from the sheer number of books, which, according to Linda, totaled over ten thousand volumes in the library and over ten thousand more throughout the house, was the ceiling.

"The ceiling is a painting by the 18th century painter Pellegrini," Linda began. "It's called *The Chariot of Aurora*. It came from a palace in Venice. It's sixty-four feet long and thirty-two feet wide."

Ellen stood gazing at the lovely depiction of the winged gods and goddesses that seemed to be riding on a chariot of clouds through a blue sky.

"What do you boys think about all those books?" Jody asked Trent and Trevor.

"Cool," Trevor said.

"Notice the small spiral staircase to the right of the fireplace?" Linda asked. "George Vanderbilt created a passageway to the second-floor bedrooms, so his guests would have easy access to his book collection, if they felt inclined to read before bed."

"Do you read before bed?" Ellen asked Trent and Trevor.

Trevor nodded, but Trent shrugged.

June mussed Trent's hair and laughed.

Ellen's attention was drawn to a man standing inside the roped-off room near the staircase flipping through a book. He was thin and of average height with short brown hair, and he was wearing a tan cardigan and navy trousers. His back was to her.

"I wonder who he is," Ellen whispered to Brian as she pointed to the man.

"Who?" Brian asked.

"That man standing over there reading," she said. "He must be important to be allowed inside the ropes."

Brian's brows knitted together. "Love, there's no one standing over there."

Ellen squinted.

The man turned to look at her and gave her a nod before he vanished.

Ellen blinked. Had she imagined him?

CHAPTER EIGHT

The Dancer in the Garden

Linda led the groom's group down the grand spiral staircase to the basement, where she showed them an old-fashioned gymnasium, an empty swimming pool made of glossy, white subway tile, and a bowling alley with two lanes. Situated between the swimming pool and bowling alley were a half dozen dressing rooms for men and an equal number for ladies. There were also several servants' rooms, the main kitchen, the servants' dining room, and laundry rooms for drying, folding, and ironing.

"It's all so *Downton Abbey*," Ellen said to Sue, who was still catching her breath from the stairs.

"*Downton* didn't have a bowling alley," Sue said. "Or a swimming pool."

"I doubt it had a gymnasium either," Tanya pointed out.

"Are you okay?" Ellen asked Sue.

"I could do without the stairs. You'd think they'd have an elevator."

"I was told they do, but it's rarely used," Maya said from behind them.

"I think I'll live," Sue said. "But if I don't, at least I'll rest easy, knowing my last day was in a beautiful place."

"You aren't dying today," Tom said. "Remember what Ted said last night? Only the good die young."

"Dad!" Lexi chastised.

"I'm just impressed that you think I'm young," Sue said to Tom.

"Only because he's older than you," Dave pointed out with a grin.

From the bowling alley, they walked through a dark, narrow passageway of brick to a large, rectangular space called the Halloween Room. The brick walls were painted with whimsical murals of witches, bats, black cats, and a platoon of wooden soldiers.

"Back in the 1920s," Linda began, "a famous theatrical troupe called *La Chauve-Souris*, which translates to *The Bat*, were seen on Broadway by the Cecils. Well, they became huge fans. They painted these murals based on the illustrations in the theatrical program and then held a gypsy-themed ball on December 30, 1925, as part of their New Year's celebration. Tonight, you will have the opportunity to see it transformed again as it becomes the venue for the dance floor."

"I can't wait," Maya whispered to Ellen.

From the basement, they climbed the grand spiral staircase and toured the second and third floors, where all the bedrooms were located. Each room had a fireplace and gorgeous furnishings, fabrics, and finishes—not to mention special Christmas décor. Most rooms also had bathrooms, though some rooms shared one at the end of a hall. Unlike the lavishly furnished bedrooms on the second and third floors, the fourth-floor servant quarters were bare, with not much more than a cot, table, and sink. Linda explained that back in the day the servants were invited to add a personal touch to their quarters by bringing their own linens and personal effects. Each floor also had a living hall. The second-floor living hall had a family portrait on one wall and, according to Linda, the two most sizable paintings were of the architect and the landscape architect hired by Vanderbilt to make his dream a reality.

Once they'd seen nearly every square foot of the house, Linda released them to explore the gardens and courtyard.

Ellen enjoyed watching Trevor and Trent chase little Bri around the gardens while she and Jody caught up on what had been going on in each other's lives. Later, Tanya asked Ellen to pose in photos with her and Sue and to snap photos of Tanya with her family. Ellen was glad that someone was thinking about taking photos.

They toured the conservatory, where Tanya took photos of things she wanted to plant in her garden. The kids were delighted by a model train and railroad track that swept across the conservatory, along with a miniature of Biltmore House and its outbuildings. Behind the conservatory was a vendor where Ellen bought Bri, Trent, and Trevor popsicles.

As they began to make their way back toward the house up the winding paths bordered by shrubs and trees, Ellen noticed a flash of pink beneath a weeping cedar tree.

Had the Pink Lady followed them to Biltmore House?

Tanya, who'd been taking a photo of Dave, noticed it too, and glanced back at Ellen with wide eyes.

When Ellen caught up to her, she asked Tanya, "Did you see that?"

"Yes. But I couldn't tell if she was a living person or a ghost. She was wearing a tutu."

Ellen frowned. "That doesn't sound like the Pink Lady."

"This was a ballerina," Tanya said. "Not a woman in a ballgown."

"Don't look at me," Dave said. "I didn't see her."

"Was she real, do you think?" Ellen asked Tanya.

"She must have been, if we both saw her."

"I mean a real, living person."

"How could she vanish into thin air if she were a living person?" Tanya glanced down at her phone.

"I suppose a real, living person wouldn't be wearing a tutu out here," Ellen conceded.

"What?" Tanya said suddenly. "My phone just died."

"Let's look for her," Ellen suggested. "Did you wear your tourmaline ring?"

"Darn. I didn't. You?"

Ellen lifted her hand to show Tanya the ring.

At that moment, Sue, Tom, and Brian caught up with them.

"What are you two up to?" Sue asked as she stopped to catch her breath. "You look kind of suspicious."

"Tanya thinks she saw a ghost," Dave explained.

"Ellen saw it, too," Tanya said. "She was a ballerina dressed in a pink tutu."

"We'll meet you guys up at the house," Ellen said to their husbands. "We want to try to spot her again."

"Don't lose track of time," Tom warned. "Sue needs more than an hour to get ready."

"That's true," Sue said with a shrug. "But I'm sure everyone appreciates the effort I make. After all, this body is a temple."

Tom smirked. "Yeah, ancient and crumbling."

"Tom!" Ellen chastised.

"She knows I'm teasing."

"Only because his temple is more ancient than mine," Sue said with a laugh.

Brian kissed Ellen's cheek and followed Dave and Tom up the hill from the gardens.

"Where did you see her?" Sue asked, once the men had gone.

Tanya led them toward the weeping cedar, in the opposite direction of Biltmore House. Not finding any sign of the ballerina from the path, they crossed under the sprawled, fringed branches of the weeping cedar, looking like something from out of a fairytale, and forayed across ground cover and through shrubs, hoping to catch sight of her. Ellen had a full-spectrum camera in her purse, which she used to scan their surroundings, but there was no sign of the ballerina she and Tanya thought they'd seen.

They hadn't wandered too far off the path when Ellen gasped. On the digital reading of the full-spectrum camera, she saw the outline of a ballerina with her arms raised over her head, about to make a turn. Ellen looked up to see a full-bodied apparition. As the thin, petite figure spun to face them, Ellen was startled by the woman's age. While her body appeared to be that of someone in her twenties, her face revealed a woman closer to Ellen's age. Ellen blinked and studied the woman again. Then the ballerina glared back at Ellen, put her finger to her lips, and danced off into the woods.

Before Ellen could ask her friends if they'd seen what she'd seen, an angry voice permeated the thick brush from the path, which was no longer in view.

The angry voice sounded like Ted Stone. He said, "Dammit, James! Why must you insist on starting something. Keep your comments to yourself."

Ellen glanced at her friends with a worried look, as James could be heard shouting, "I don't start trouble, I finish it. You started it decades ago. So don't go blaming me."

The three friends edged closer to the path to get a better view.

"Let it go, Ted," Gayle insisted. "Just ignore him."

"Keep your mouth shut, James," Melissa demanded. "Everyone's had enough."

"At least we agree on one thing," Ted said angrily.

"No need to shout at *me*," Melissa said to Ted.

"That's what assholes do," James insisted. "They blame others for their own mistakes."

"Let's just leave," Gayle said to Ted. "Maya won't miss us."

"She damn sure will!" Ted cried. "We can't do that to her."

"Just leave us alone," Gayle said to James. "For Maya's sake."

"Tell your husband," James argued. "He approached me first."

"Only because of your damn comments," Ted insisted.

Ellen felt sick. Would their bickering never end?

She was grateful when Greg, Maya's dad, came upon the feuding grandparents and broke them up.

"We need to get dressed, Dad," Greg said to Ted. "You and Mom come with me. I'll show you to your room."

"And I'll show you to yours," Karen said to her parents. "But let's sit here on this bench for a moment and regain our composure."

"My composure's fine," James insisted, but he followed his daughter to the bench, anyway.

Ellen turned to her friends and whispered, "Pray that they don't ruin Lane's wedding. If they do, I swear there will be four more ghosts haunting Biltmore."

Sue and Ellen had caught up with their husbands, who were looking at an outdoor display of an enlarged map of Biltmore Estate in front of the library terrace. Brian, however, was not with them, so Ellen continued along the front terrace and past the main entrance in search of him. She was alarmed when she discovered Lane standing by himself near the shuttle drop-off point near a cluster of trees. He was wiping his eyes and appeared to be crying. Ellen's stomach formed a knot. Why would Lane be crying on his wedding day?

She was about to approach him when she saw Brian had beat her to it. She was close enough to overhear them, but they didn't see her there on the other side of the trees. She decided to eavesdrop.

"What's up, Lane? Everything okay?" Brian asked.

"I'm just missing my dad, that's all."

Ellen put her hand on her heart and began fighting her own tears.

"I understand. My dad died young, too. I was even younger than you. It sucks, and I'm sorry."

"Yeah, it does."

"Your mom believes he's here in spirit. I think I believe that, too. What about you?" Brian asked.

Lane nodded. "Yeah, I guess so. I just wish I could talk to him and ask him stuff. You know?"

Ellen wiped her eyes with the back of her hands. She wished she could have been both mother and father in Paul's absence, but there's no replacing a father.

"Yeah, I get it," Brian said. "I hope you know you can ask me stuff—that is, if you feel like I might know the answers."

Lane nodded. "I'm just wanting advice, man to man. I'm wondering what he would say about trying to keep a wife happy, about making a marriage successful. He and my mom were married for a really long time."

"That's true," Brian said. "And I've only been married to your mother for two years. But I do think I've learned something that might help you."

"Really? What?"

Ellen was curious to know, too.

"Well, let's see. How can I put it? Oh, here we go. When you DJ, you combine elements from two different records to make a new sound, but you must sometimes slow one record down, or find the right part to blend them together. You have to listen to both records to make this new sound, right?"

"Yeah. I think I see where you're going with that."

"It's hard to listen to both beats, both melodies, and fuse them together. Sometimes one record goes faster or slower than the other, or the beat of one song might dominate the beat of another. It's hard to get them in sync together, isn't it?"

"It's an art, that's for sure."

"The key is to listen," he said. "If you ever feel like you're out of sync with one another, listen to what she's saying. Sometimes she doesn't say it with words, but you still must listen. And if you can't hear what's missing, then you must ask."

"I like that, man," Lane said. "It makes sense. Thank you."

"Glad I could help."

Ellen was moved that Brian could be there for Lane. She was proud of what he'd said and felt Paul would have approved.

"How has it been, being married to my mom?" Lane asked. "Are you happy?"

"I don't think I've ever been happier, to tell you the truth," he said. "It hasn't always been easy between us. We've had to figure each other out—each other's rhythms and melodies and beats."

"You've done a great job at extending that metaphor," Lane said with a laugh.

"I do my best." Brian laughed, too. "But in all seriousness, we struggled in the beginning with how much time we each needed to be together and apart. She's more independent than any woman I've ever been with. That took some getting used to."

Ellen smiled, pleased that he hadn't been too frustrated with her.

"It was the same for Maya," Lane said. "We almost broke up when we were first dating because she wanted to spend every free day we had together. But I guess I'm like my mom. I need a lot of alone time and time to do my own thing. I was relieved that Maya came to understand that. But I don't want her to feel neglected, either. This marriage isn't just about what I need and what I want. We have to find a balance."

"That's exactly right. And you might teeter and totter for a while before you find it, but you will. Hell, Lane, I can already tell just listening to you that you're going to make an excellent husband."

"Thanks, Brian. That means a lot."

"I think so, too," Maya said as she caught up to them from the area where the lockers and restrooms were located. Lane must have been waiting for her to use the facilities. Ellen decided to catch up with them, too.

"Hi there," Ellen said. "I think the house has been closed to the public and it's time to go in and get changed. Are y'all ready?"

"Sure am," Maya said with a smile. "What about you, Lane?"

"No, dude. Let's get out of here. I'm not ready for this."

"What?" Ellen cried.

Lane cracked up laughing. "You're too easy, Mom. Of course, I'm ready. Let's go."

CHAPTER NINE

The Wedding

Ellen stood beside Brian on the front lawn of the Biltmore Estate as the string quartet began to play the wedding march. She felt pretty in her champagne gown, made of lace and a fine knit, loosely sheathing her body all the way to the floor. It had a scoop neck and a cinched waist that flattered her figure, though, even with the matching shawl, she was cold.

Maya and her father arrived in a horse-drawn carriage on the paved path normally used by the shuttles. The carriage came to a halt a few yards from the carpeted aisle, where Greg helped Maya down before escorting her toward the arbor of white roses and tulle, where Lane and the rest of the wedding party were already waiting with the minister.

Maya's dress was stunning. She wore a white faux fur draped over her shoulders. It fell to just above her waist, where the bodice met the long, white skirt and lace train. She also wore a tiara with a white tulle veil that fell just past her chestnut, shoulder-length hair, and she carried a bouquet of white roses.

Lane looked smart in his charcoal tux, as did Nolan, who stood beside him as his best man. Alison looked beautiful where she stood with the other bridesmaids in their form-fitting lavender gowns.

When it was time for Lane to recite his vows, Ellen's tears couldn't be contained. She was full of too many emotions to rein them back a moment longer. Most of all, she was happy for her son. Brian curled an arm around her waist and pulled her close to him.

She was relieved when the minister pronounced Lane and Maya husband and wife. The ceremony had been a great success. Nothing had gone wrong. No ghosts or grandparents had interfered.

After the wedding party proceeded down the aisle, they and the parents and grandparents were escorted across the expansive lawn past the fountain and enormous Christmas tree to the *rampe douce*, or double ramp, to the esplanade that overlooked Biltmore. At the far end of the esplanade was the temple of Diana.

The photographers took dozens of photos of Lane and Maya and the wedding party facing Diana's temple with the Biltmore House in the background while the rest of the wedding guests were directed to cocktails on the library terrace. Ellen couldn't help but worry that the feuding grandparents would start bickering again there on the esplanade, but Greg and Karen seemed to be doing a good job of keeping them apart.

Then, as everyone squeezed together for one final shot, it began to snow. It was a soft, fluffy snow, and the landscape quickly became covered with it, turning an already remarkable landscape into something supremely beautiful. The photographer recommended that the couple allow her to take a few more shots while the others headed for the library terrace, which was quite a long walk. But, as Ellen was descending the *rampe douce,* she saw a flash of pink in the corner of her eye. She turned to gaze at the temple of Diana and was stunned to see the ghostly ballerina dancing there.

Not sure whether she should continue with the rest of the guests toward the house or investigate the temple, Ellen stopped in her tracks, twisting her tourmaline ring on her finger.

"What's wrong?" Brian asked.

"Would you mind walking with me to the temple, to look at the statue of Diana?"

"Not at all, but aren't you cold?"

"A little, but I'll be alright."

Now that she and Brian were approaching the temple, the ballerina was no longer in sight. The statue of Diana with her hound was worth the walk, however. It was perched on a foundation of bricks beneath a vine-covered arbor made of wood. The arbor rested on six stone columns that reminded Ellen of Greece. Brian took Ellen by the hand and led her under the arbor beside the statue where he wrapped her in his arms and kissed her.

"I've been wanting to do that all day," he said softly.

She smiled. "I'm glad you finally did."

He kissed her again, passionately, and, for a second, she forgot herself. But when she caught a flash of that pink tutu again, she flinched.

"What's wrong?" he asked.

"I saw the ghost again, but she's disappeared."

He glanced around and, seeing nothing, said, "Should we head back?"

"Not yet." She leaned in for one more lingering kiss before saying, "Okay. Let's go."

He took her hand and grinned as they walked together toward the *rampe douce*, where Lane and Maya were just finishing up with the photographer.

With Lane and Maya, Ellen and Brian strolled down the double ramp toward the Christmas tree, past the fountain, and past the rows of white chairs. It took them ten minutes to reach the façade of the house. Then they continued up the steps to the library terrace, where the rest of the wedding party were having cocktails and snacks. When they saw the arrival of the bride and groom, the guests applauded, and someone even whistled. Then Patricia opened the library doors and led the group into Biltmore House.

The absence of ropes and tourists gave the house an entirely different ambience. It somehow felt more intimate and less museum-like. Patricia led them to the tapestry gallery, where a guest registry book and portrait of the bride had been set up near the wedding cakes. Beside the registry, a decorated box for wedding cards was on display for any who wished to leave a card for the bride and groom. A line formed to sign the book. Once Sue and Tanya had signed for their families, Ellen walked with them to admire the cakes. The bride's three-tiered cake was ivory with white roses on each tier and white pearl beads around the base. The groom's cake was chocolate and shaped like a vinyl record sitting on a turn table. Ellen didn't know that this was what Lane and Maya had chosen. It made her smile.

Tanya and Sue were wearing the gorgeous gowns they had bought last year when the three of them had shopped together at the Red Carpet Boutique in New Orleans while solving the case of the ghost of Blackfeet Nation. Tanya's gown was by Mac Duggal. It had an asymmetric neckline and was made of chiffon with a red blossom print on a light gray background and a single sheer set-in bell sleeve. Sue wore an off-shoulder Tiffany in gold and black brocade with angel sleeves and a drop waist. She looked like a mermaid princess. Like Ellen, they carried clutches just large enough for their phone, key, and a tube of lipstick.

Patricia led the guests through the main hall and winter garden into the banquet hall, where the thirty-seven-foot Christmas tree with its five hundred lights towered over them in front of the long copper pipes of an organ, along with two round chandeliers hanging from the wooden barrel ceiling seventy feet above. Fires danced inside the triple limestone fireplace on the opposite side of the room, and along the back wall were mounted heads of deer, elk, and antelope.

Ellen glanced at the name cards on the tables as people were finding their seats. Lane and Maya were seated at the center of the long table. She and Brian had seats next to the groom. Ted and Gayle Stone sat on the bride's side next to Karen, but James and Melissa Dresden sat on the groom's side next to Brian. Given what had already transpired between the two sets of grandparents, Ellen found this to be smart planning. Jody and his family sat on the other side of the Dresdens. The bridesmaids and groomsmen sat with their partners on the opposite side of the long table. Two extra tables had been brought in to accommodate overflow. Sue and Tanya and their families were assigned to one while Gordon and Lou Cinda, Mike and Marcia, and Maya's aunt and uncle were assigned to the other.

Before taking her seat, Ellen went to check on her friends. They were seated next to the triple fireplace, which had cozy flames dancing in each of the limestone hearths.

"Are y'all doing okay?" she asked them.

Sue shrugged. "I don't know, we're in America's largest privately owned home—some even call it a castle—staying the night in luxurious rooms that haven't been slept in for decades, though you wouldn't know it by how clean everything is. And we're about to be served in a banquet hall that's literally fit for a king. I guess we're okay, wouldn't you say Tanya?"

"I think we're okay," Tanya said.

"Though," Sue began again, "we might want to wait and see how the food is before we cast our final verdict."

"Mom!" Lexi chastised.

Ellen leaned close to her friends and said, "I saw her again."

"The ballerina?" Tanya asked. "Where?"

"Near Diana's temple on the esplanade. I think she wanted me to see her."

"Do you think this is who the spa ghost warned you about?" Tanya asked.

Ellen shrugged.

"Maybe tonight we'll have time to reach out," Sue said.

Ellen had taken a few strides toward her table when a man in an old-fashioned tux stopped her and, dabbing his watering eyes with a hand-kerchief, said, "Can you help me?"

"We haven't met," Ellen said, concerned by his tears. "Are you a relative of Maya's?"

He gave her a puzzled look. "Who is Maya?"

"Are you not a guest?" She gave him a once over, wondering if he was a server, though his tux was different from what the others were wearing. It was more old-fashioned.

"I was the very first guest on the registry," he said.

He handed her a folded piece of paper before literally fading into thin air.

Ellen clung to the paper with shaking hands. Her knees felt weak, and she had to grab onto the back of someone else's chair to keep herself from falling.

"Mom?" Nolan asked as he stood from his seat. "Are you okay?"

She took a deep breath and nodded. When he reached her, she whispered, "I just saw another ghost. I don't know what's going on. This *never* happens."

Nolan helped her back to her seat. "Maybe you should take a break from all the paranormal stuff."

She gave him a smile but said nothing as she sat beside Brian.

"Is red okay?" Brian asked her. "I wasn't sure what to tell the server."

"Perfect," she said before taking a large gulp of wine.

Then she opened the folded piece of paper with trembling hands and read: *Meet me beside the swimming pool at ten o'clock tonight. I have something important to say.*

Ellen leaned close to Brian. "I'll be right back."

Without further explanation, she left the room, crossed through the winter garden and main hall, and entered the tapestry gallery, where she searched through the guest registry. Written on the very first line was "Sue and Tom Graham." So, what had the weeping man meant when he'd claimed to have been the first guest on the registry?

Ellen returned to her seat in the banquet hall beside Brian and Lane, where the tender pork crown roast, sauteed potatoes and green beans, and crispy garlic toast soon replaced any thoughts of the weeping man. Shortly after she had finished her meal, she was delighted by Nolan's speech as the best man. It made her eyes water all over again. Although Jen's speech as the maid of honor was less brief and less emotional, it had them all in stitches.

Ellen was relieved when neither grandfather stood to speak, and Patricia, the wedding coordinator, invited the guests to follow her to the tapestry gallery for the cutting of the cake. The photographer took a few photos of the bride and groom as the guests were invited to sit on the blue upholstered chairs and couches arranged about the long rectangular room with its two gorgeous fireplaces and five Christmas trees. Ellen sat with Brian and Tanya and Sue and their husbands, where they were served coffee and hot tea. Once the photographer was finished, cake was served as well.

When Ellen saw Shiri among the servers, she excused herself and crossed the room to show her the note she'd received from the weeping man.

"That's impressive," Shiri said. "It takes quite a lot of energy for a ghost to write a note, manifest himself, and speak."

Ellen frowned. "You don't believe me?"

"I believe you. It's the full moon. It gives the spirits more power."

"I hadn't thought of that."

"And I know who he is," Shiri said. "He talks to me all the time, and he's like a broken record."

Ellen lifted her brows. "Who is he?"

"Gallatin Roberts," Shiri whispered. "He was the mayor of Asheville in the 1920s but was forced to resign in 1930 after the bank failed with millions of city funds on deposit. He was indicted in 1931 for misallocating public money."

"Was he guilty?" Ellen asked.

She shrugged. "He claimed his innocence in his suicide note."

"He committed suicide? Oh, my gosh."

"He shot himself in his office above the bank."

Ellen covered her mouth, thanked Shiri, and returned to her seat with Brian and her friends.

"We may have some work to do tonight," she said to Sue and Tanya. "Are you up for it?"

"We said we might we reach out to the ballerina," Sue said.

"Yes, but there's another ghost that needs our help," Ellen explained.

"When? Now?" Tanya asked.

"Ten o'clock," Ellen said. "At the swimming pool after the dance."

"Is it really necessary?" Brian asked with a frown.

"I think it's worth checking out." Ellen went on to tell them what she'd learned from Shiri. "Maybe there's something we can do to help him to find peace. He's been trapped here since 1931."

Brian pecked her on the cheek. "You're right. It's worth looking into. But promise me a dance before you go."

"You got it," she said with a grin.

From the tapestry room, Patricia led the guests back to the main hall, to the grand spiral staircase, where they descended to the basement. They followed her down a narrow stone corridor, alight with faux candles lining the pathway, to the Halloween Room, which had been transformed with strands of white lights, white tulle, and white roses, along with white petals strewn about the floor. A band was set up in one corner. One of the members, a man in his twenties, held a microphone and invited everyone to gather in a circle so the bride and groom could share their first dance.

When the music began, Brian wrapped an arm around Ellen's waist as they watched Lane and Maya dance together. Ellen was filled with joy as she watched Lane gazing down at his lovely bride. After several minutes, the mother of the groom and father of the bride were invited to dance with their respective children. Ellen beamed up at Lane, who hadn't stopped smiling all day.

"You look happy," she said to him.

"I've never been happier, Mom," he said before he kissed her on the cheek.

She cocked her head to one side. "Promise me you'll visit often."

"Are you crying again?"

"No. Well, maybe a little bit." She sniffed.

"We'll visit often. I promise."

When the song ended, Brian approached to dance the next one with Ellen while Lane danced with Karen Stone.

They hadn't been dancing long when all the strands of little white lights went out at once, along with the sconces on the walls, and they were bathed in darkness.

"Don't panic," the leader of the band called out over the gasps and murmurs of the wedding guests. "We'll get the electricity back on momentarily. Meanwhile, please stay where you are."

Brian used the light on his phone to guide Ellen across the room to Patricia.

"What's going on?" he asked the wedding coordinator.

"I've called maintenance, and they're looking into it," she said. "Please be patient. This is an old house and things like this sometimes happen."

"Does it happen often?" Ellen asked her.

"Not really," Patricia admitted. "Hold on. I'm getting a call."

Patricia put her phone to her ear. "Patricia here."

Brian and Ellen waited as the wedding coordinator spoke to someone on the other end. Then Ellen felt a cold chill, and the hair on the back of her neck stood on end. Her mouth and eyes grew wide as, across the room in the darkness, a white orb floated over the crowd toward her. She held her breath as the orb drew near and the translucent face of a young woman appeared, along with a hand. The index finger pointed at Ellen and then turned and beckoned her.

"Who are you?" Ellen asked.

Brian turned to her. "Love? Who are you talking to?"

Ellen watched in astonishment as the orb floated away from her, over the crowd, and disappeared. As soon as the orb had vanished, the lights came back on.

"There we go," the band leader said into his microphone.

The room burst into happy applause.

"And a one, two, three, four."

The music resumed, as did the dancing.

"I'll be right back," Ellen said to Brian.

"Where are you going?" he asked.

"After another ghost."

He nodded as she squeezed his shoulder. Then she went looking for Sue and Tanya.

CHAPTER TEN

A Ghostly Plea

Ellen led Sue and Tanya from the Halloween Room through the door where she had last seen the orb to the ladies' dressing rooms. They walked through a narrow hall with dressing stalls to their left and a sitting room at the end. On the sofa in front of a crackling fire sat Melissa Dresden in tears.

"Melissa?" Ellen asked. "Are you okay?"

Melissa shrugged. "I'm just so tired of it all."

Sue sat on the chair across from the sofa. "Tired of what?"

"The fighting. It's ancient history, but every time we're forced together, it all comes back so painfully."

Ellen sat on the arm of Sue's chair. "Do you want to talk about it? Or would you rather be left alone?"

They were interrupted when Lou Cinda, Paul's sister-in-law, exited one of the bathrooms off the sitting room.

"Oh, hello," she said. "Ellen, I've been meaning to tell you how beautiful the ceremony was. And this house is incredible. Thank you so much for including Gordon and me."

Ellen lifted her chin. "You're part of our family. We're so glad you could be here for Lane's special day."

Lou Cinda smiled. "Thanks, Ellen. Aren't you coming back to the dance?"

"I'll be there in a moment," Ellen said.

Once Lou Cinda left the ladies' dressing rooms, Ellen turned to Melissa. "We're here if you need someone to talk to."

"I'm not sure how talking will help anything," she said. "But thank you for the offer."

In that moment, the lights overhead flickered and went out. So did the white lights on a small Christmas tree beside the fireplace and on another strand draped across the mantle. The fire in the hearth provided just enough light for them to see by.

"What's going on with the electricity in this place?" Tanya wondered out loud.

"I d-don't think the problem is a mechanical one," Sue stammered as she pointed to the ceiling.

Ellen looked up to see the white orb that had appeared to her in the Halloween Room. The hair on the back of her neck stood up, and goosebumps covered her arms. No matter how often she saw a ghost, she found it unnerving.

"Oh my gosh," Tanya whispered.

"What's the matter?" Melissa asked. "What do you see?"

"It's the face of a young woman inside of a white orb," Ellen explained.

"You mean a ghost?"

The three friends nodded as a chill filled the air despite the blazing fire in the hearth.

"You can't see it?" Tanya asked Melissa.

Melissa shook her head.

Ellen wished she had her full-spectrum camera. If she could capture an image of the woman in the orb, Melissa might be more inclined to believe.

"Have you come to talk to us?" Sue asked the orb.

The head inside the orb nodded.

"We're listening," Ellen said. "Please say whatever you've come to say."

The hand appeared inside the orb and pointed to Ellen, just as it had in the Halloween Room.

"Does she want something from you, Ellen?" Tanya asked.

"I have no idea."

The orb disappeared. Ellen and her friends glanced around, to see where she had gone, but there was no sign of her.

Ellen flinched when her clutch was knocked from her hand and her phone, key, and lipstick fell to the rug near her feet. She froze in shocked silence when her phone levitated a few inches in the air before falling again.

"What the hell?" Melissa stood up and backed away from the phone. "Is this some kind of trick?"

Tanya snapped her fingers. "She wants you to use the ghost app."

"Oh, I bet that's it," Sue agreed.

With trembling hands, Ellen opened the app, and white noise filled the room.

"My name . . ." the app began.

"What's your name?" Sue asked eagerly.

"Melinda," the ghost app said.

Melissa covered her mouth and said, "Stop this. It isn't funny."

"Brown," the app added.

"Please tell me that this is a joke." More tears filled Melissa's eyes.

"It isn't a joke," Ellen said. "It's what we do. It seems your sister wants to speak with you."

"Listen," the ghost app said.

Melissa crossed her arms over her chest. "How do you know my sister's name? You planned this."

"This isn't a joke or a trick," Sue insisted. "One of the servers told us that Melinda haunts Biltmore House and talks to her all the time."

"That's right," Ellen said. "She said that Melinda can't find peace until you tell your family the truth about what happened."

Melissa gawked. For several seconds, she stared at them in silence. Then she said, "You don't know what you're talking about."

"Please," the ghost app said. "Tell . . . the truth."

Melissa pulled her shawl more tightly around herself and stormed from the room.

The orb appeared and followed her.

"Wait!" Sue cried. "Please stay and tell us what happened."

But both Melissa and the orb fled from the dressing rooms as the lights flickered back to life.

"What should we do now?" Tanya wondered.

"Let's follow them and see if the orb stays with Melissa," Sue suggested.

"I need to pee," Ellen said. "Will you wait for me?"

Tanya followed. "I should go, too."

"Well, I don't want to be left out of all the fun," Sue teased as she made her way to the third stall.

Once they'd finished using the restroom, the three friends returned to the Halloween Room in search of the white orb and Melissa Dresden, but neither sister could be found.

Brian crossed the room for another dance. Ellen enjoyed it while keeping her eye out for Melissa Dresden. Ellen meant to go looking for the woman when the song ended, but the band leader announced that it was time for the Chicken Dance.

Ellen couldn't get Sue and Tom to join in, but Tanya and Dave did, as did almost everyone else. Ellen smiled to see her family members having fun together, and she wished she weren't so anxious to get away. As soon as the Chicken Dance ended, the Hokey Pokey began. After that, they danced the Shottish, and then the Cotton-Eyed Joe.

Once the string of dances had finally come to an end, and since there was still no sign of Melissa Dresden, Ellen rounded up Tanya and Sue to go on a search.

Lane had just tossed the garter to the bachelors in the room—little Trent and Trevor, Sue's twenty-two-year-old son Luke, and Lane's friends Jeffrey and Curtis. The garter bounced off Luke's chest and landed on the floor, where it was snatched up by Trevor.

"That shows you how eager Luke is to settle down," Sue murmured.

The three friends waited as Maya turned to toss her bouquet. Sammy, Jen, Alison, and Cammie were lined up, none looking eager to catch the flowers. The bouquet landed squarely in Alison's arms.

Ellen crossed the room to hug her daughter.

"Don't get your hopes up," Alison said to her. "I'm not even dating anyone."

"This could be a good sign that you're about to meet someone," Ellen reassured her.

Alison rolled her eyes and walked away.

Ellen finally spotted James, Melissa's husband, and crossed the room to speak with him. "Have you seen Melissa?"

"She needed some fresh air. She went upstairs to one of the terraces."

"Thanks," Ellen said.

Because other guests had also left the dance to venture to other parts of the house, Ellen and her friends didn't look conspicuous as they ascended the spiral staircase in search of Melissa.

At the top of the stairs, they found a door leading to a terrace that overlooked the front lawn of Biltmore, where the white chairs, arbor, carpeted aisle, and black iron gate had been removed and there was nothing but a blanket of snow between the fountain and the house. Snowflakes continued to drop from the night sky.

"I can't believe it's still snowing," Ellen said from the terrace, where they'd found no sign of Melissa. "It's freezing out here."

"Look how beautiful it is," Tanya said with a sigh.

Even the large Christmas tree on the other side of the fountain was covered in snow, its twinkling bright lights barely shining through its white, fluffy blanket.

"Come on," Sue said as she headed back inside.

They crossed the main hall to the tapestry gallery, where a few other guests sat eating cake and sipping hot cups of coffee. Nolan and Taylor were among them, Taylor sitting on a chair with a sleeping Bri in her arms.

When Ellen approached them, Nolan said, "We're about to turn in for the night."

"Already?" Tanya asked.

"It's way past Bri's bedtime," he explained.

Ellen kissed Nolan's cheek and the top of Taylor's head. "Goodnight. See you at breakfast in the morning."

Sue led them from the tapestry room out onto the back terrace overlooking the Blue Ridge Mountains, visible beneath a nearly full moon. They, too, were covered in snow.

"There she is," Tanya said, nodding toward the end of the terrace, where they had first entered Biltmore before their tour earlier that day.

They strolled over to where Melissa stood huddled beside one of the columns, leaning on the stone railing.

"Aren't you cold out here?" Ellen asked her.

"I just needed a breather," she said as she turned toward them. "But you're right. It's too cold to stay out here for long. I think I'll go inside."

They followed her through the nearest entrance, which happened to lead to the library.

Ellen's attention was immediately drawn to the Pellegrini painting on the ceiling, the winged gods floating on their chariot of clouds. Then, a figure on the second-floor balcony near the bookshelf caught her eye. It was the man in the tan cardigan and navy slacks. As before, he gave her a nod and vanished.

Ellen shivered. This was too bizarre.

To Tanya, she whispered, "Did you see that?"

"See what?" she whispered back.

Ellen shook her head. "Never mind."

Melissa took a seat on one of the burgundy damask sofas in front of the black marble fireplace, where another fire crackled in the hearth. Ellen wondered how many people it took to clean so many fireplaces.

"We don't want to impose," Sue began as she stood hovering over Melissa. "But we promise we weren't tricking you earlier. Your sister wants to find peace, and you have the power to make that happen."

"The truth shall set you free," Ellen said with a smile. "It can't be that bad, can it?"

Melissa pulled her shawl more tightly around her arms. "It's hurtful. People will be hurt."

"Who?" Tanya asked.

"Ted for one. And James. It might even hurt Gayle. I don't know."

"Aren't they already hurting because of this ongoing feud?" Sue pointed out.

"The truth will only make it worse," Melissa said.

"Even if it means your sister will finally find peace?" Ellen asked.

Melissa looked up at Ellen and studied her.

Ellen blushed. "We're only trying to help. I promise. We've helped others in the past."

"That's why the ghosts seek us out," Sue explained. "They can sense our gifts. We've refined them over the years."

"Is she here now?" Melissa asked. "Melinda?"

Ellen and her friends glanced around the room.

"I can't see her," Ellen said. "But that doesn't mean she isn't here. She followed you when you left the ladies' dressing rooms."

Melissa's eyes widened. "I thought I felt her outside on the terrace. When we were young, we used to give each other butterfly kisses. That's where you blink close enough to the other's face so that your eyelashes caress the other's cheek. Anyway, I could have sworn I felt her lashes on my cheek out there."

"It sounds like you were close," Tanya said from where she sat near the fire.

"We were best friends."

"How did she die?" Sue asked.

Melissa clenched her teeth, fighting tears, before she said, "She overdosed. I think it was intentional, but I don't know for sure."

"I'm so sorry," Ellen said.

"That's so sad," Tanya added. "Why do you think it was intentional?"

"Because she was in love with Ted," Melissa said through her tears. "And he was in love with me."

Ellen glanced at her friends, not sure what to say.

Before she or they could think of anything, Melissa continued, "Everyone thinks I was left at the altar by Ted, because he didn't want to marry me." She sniffled. "But the truth is, we loved each other deeply. A few days before our wedding, I convinced him that I didn't love him as much as a wife should love a husband, but it was a lie. I did it because I could see how poorly my sister was, and I knew I'd be miserable, too, if I went through with it."

"She might have moved on," Sue suggested.

Melissa shook her head. "I don't think so. She had it bad for him. A few days before the wedding, I persuaded Ted to leave me standing at the altar, because I knew my parents would disown me if they knew it was me breaking it off. Everyone was shocked when he didn't show up. Before I had a chance to explain things to Melinda, she assumed Ted hadn't loved me after all. She went to him, eager to win him over. She hadn't even waited a day. He rejected her, and that night, the night that should have been my wedding night, she overdosed."

"Oh, no," Ellen said. "I'm so sorry."

"But I don't understand why this has caused a decades-long feud with Ted and Gayle," Sue said.

"Ted is bitter. He thinks I treated him unfairly—and he's right. He doesn't know that it nearly killed me to give him up. The truth is, I still love him. I never stopped loving him."

Ellen sucked in her lips. She finally understood why Melissa had been protecting the truth.

"James had always been in love with me, even when Ted and I were engaged. When Ted didn't show up on our wedding day, James, who was a groomsman for Ted, went ballistic. He couldn't believe that Ted could hurt me like that. And he won't let it go, and this only worsens Ted's frustration, because he, of course, was not the one who hurt me. I hurt him."

"He's kept your secret all these years?" Tanya asked.

"I'm not sure what he's told Gayle, but yes."

"Why do you suppose Melinda can't move on?" Ellen wondered. "Do you think she feels guilty for the pain she's caused Ted?"

The lights overhead in the library and on the Christmas tree beside the marble fireplace began to flicker.

Melissa jumped to her feet. "What's happening?"

"I don't know," Ellen admitted.

"There she is." Sue pointed to the second-floor balcony, where Ellen had seen the man in the tan cardigan and navy slacks.

It was the white orb containing the young woman's face. It was only there for a moment before it disappeared, and the lights stopped flickering.

Melissa was white-faced and trembling. Her hand covered her mouth. "Melinda?" She turned to the others. "I saw her."

Ellen glanced with excitement toward her friends. "That's wonderful. Now you know we weren't lying."

Melissa stood there for several seconds, staring at the second-floor balcony, before she finally returned to the sofa. "I knew you weren't lying. I just couldn't accept it."

"I have an idea," Tanya said. "What if you tell Ted the truth? James doesn't need to know, but maybe what your sister needs is to give Ted closure."

The lights flickered. Ellen glanced around, looking for the orb, but it did not reappear.

"If Ted knows the truth," Sue added, "James's comments will no longer hurt him."

Ellen sat beside Melissa on the sofa. "Unless you think this confession will break up the marriages. Then you might want to rethink this."

"I won't leave James. While it's true that I never stopped loving Ted—he'll always have a place in my heart—James and I have built a life together. We have children and grandchildren. We love one another. And Ted clearly loves Gayle."

"Then you should tell him," Ellen said. "I wonder why you haven't already."

"I didn't think my sister wanted him to know. But, if she wants him to hear the truth . . . I'm terrified, though. I don't know what he'll say or what he'll think of me."

"It can't be worse than it is now," Sue pointed out.

Melissa took a deep breath and nodded. "Okay. I'll do it for my sister."

CHAPTER ELEVEN

Poolside Séance

At a quarter to ten, Ellen, Tanya, and Sue met in the south hall of the second floor outside of their rooms. Ellen carried her shoulder bag containing the REM-POD, candles, matches, salt, an EMF detector, and a flashlight, along with her phone and room key. Tanya brought the Ouija Board and a tool that was both a thermometer and an EMF detector.

"What did *you* bring?" Ellen asked Sue, who appeared empty-handed.

Sue patted her crossbody bag and said, "My gun."

"Why would we need a gun, Sue? These are ghosts. They're already dead," Tanya pointed out as they crossed the hall to the grand spiral staircase, where a few other wedding guests were also meandering.

"Better safe than sorry," she replied. Then, stopping at the top of the stairs, she added, "I don't think I can do stairs anymore tonight. Can we please look for the elevator?"

"Okay," Ellen said. "This way."

Ellen led them from the staircase to the second-floor living hall and hung a right.

"The elevator should be straight ahead," Ellen said, worried about the time. She didn't want Gallatin Roberts to think they weren't coming. "Here it is."

She pushed a button. They heard the whirring and knocking of an elevator arriving. Then it stopped, but the door didn't open.

"I think you just pull it like this," Ellen said, sliding the door to one side.

"Are we certain this is safe?" Tanya asked.

Sue stepped inside. "Nothing in life is certain."

The elevator was small with barely enough room for the three of them. Wooden wainscoting reached partway up the elevator walls. The upper half was structured with decorative iron work and was otherwise open to the limestone shaft. The slowest elevator Ellen had ever ridden in, it whirred and knocked as it descended.

"Are you wearing your tourmaline rings?" Ellen asked her friends.

Tanya lifted her hand to show she was wearing hers.

"I forgot mine," Sue said. "But I'm wearing my *gris gris* in my bra." Sue looked down her dress. "I'm not sure where it went, but it's down there somewhere."

Tanya shook her head and laughed.

When the elevator stopped, Ellen slid the door open.

Tanya stepped out and looked both ways. "This doesn't look familiar."

They walked through a storeroom that was situated beneath the spiral staircase.

"Where are we?" Sue wanted to know.

"The swimming pool should be straight ahead." Ellen led them into what appeared to be another storage room filled with Christmas decorations, furniture, paintings, and books.

As they passed through yet another storage room, they heard a clatter and a thud.

The three friends froze and glanced at one another nervously.

"What the heck was that?" Sue wanted to know.

"Let's not hang around to find out," Ellen said.

"I'm with you." Tanya followed Ellen as she scurried down the hall.

"Wait for me," Sue complained. "I have bad feet, remember? You two seem to always forget that I was shot in Tulsa."

"How could we, when you remind us so often?" Tanya chided.

"We must be in a sub-basement," Ellen concluded when the bowling alley, swimming pool, and gymnasium were nowhere in sight. "Let's go back to the elevator and go up a level."

"So much for saving my feet," Sue said. "We may as well have taken the stairs. We'd be there by now."

"Oh, stop," Ellen said. "You're the one that wanted the elevator."

"I know, and I appreciate you. I just like to complain every now and then."

"No," Tanya said sarcastically. "I've never heard a complaint from *you*, Sue Graham."

They found an office with an opened door. A sign on the door read, "Authorized Personnel Only." The room held a computer, file cabinet, and shelves. To the left of the office was a large boiler room.

"This isn't right," Tanya said. "We're turned around."

"Let's go back the same way we came," Ellen suggested.

"Easy for you to say," Sue said. "You're not the one with the bad feet."

On the way back, they passed a service elevator.

Stopping in front of it, Ellen pointed to it and said, "Should we try going up in this?"

"I don't know," Tanya said with a shake of her head. "How do we know it works?"

"There'd be a sign on it if it didn't," Sue argued. "I vote we take this one."

Ellen opened the door, and they stepped inside. Although it wasn't as fancy as the main elevator near the spiral staircase, it was much larger. She pushed the button for one floor up.

As it knocked and whirred during the gradual ascent, Ellen said, "I thought the last one was slow."

"It beats following you through the labyrinth," Sue said. "All we needed was the Minotaur."

"I heard something down there," Tanya said. "Maybe it was him."

When the elevator came to a halt, Ellen pulled the door open.

"This is more like it," Tanya said once she was out in the hall. "I recognize the servants' dining room and main kitchen."

"This way," Ellen said, taking the lead.

She took them down one hall after another until she came upon the gymnasium and swimming pool. According to her phone, it was exactly ten o'clock.

"This is where he said to meet," she said, pointing at the empty pool. Lights where the pool walls met the pool floor illuminated the white subway tile all the way around. "But I don't see him anywhere. Do you?"

"I think we should conduct our séance," Sue said. "He might need help manifesting himself."

"He was full-bodied when he approached me in the banquet hall," Ellen said.

"But that takes a lot of energy," Sue argued. "Spirits have to find sources of energy, or they can't appear or make sounds."

Ellen knew that, but she said nothing in reply. She wished she'd ask Shiri to join them, since a medium can see spirits without them having to manifest themselves. Ellen had wanted to invite her but worried the server and shop owner was tired from working all day. She hadn't wanted to impose.

"Want to set up over there?" Tanya pointed to the back of the wooden deck, which surrounded the pool. "There are chairs behind that platform."

A wooden structure in the deep end that once served as a diving platform and ladder had a deck behind it with two potted palms, a bench, and two wooden chairs. The three friends walked around the pool to the back and got comfortable before lighting their candles and sprinkling a circle of protection with salt.

Ellen turned on the REM-POD and set it on the deck a few feet from where they sat. "Shall we try using the ghost app?"

"It's worked so far," Sue pointed out.

Ellen took out her phone, but no sooner had she opened the app than her phone died.

"Great," she said. "It's dead."

"Should I download the app?" Tanya offered. She took out her phone and searched for it. "I don't seem to be getting any service down here."

Sue took out her phone but had the same problem.

"He said he wanted to tell us something important," Ellen said. "Let's see if he appears and can talk. If not, we'll try something else."

The three friends held hands.

"You lead this time, Ellen," Sue said. "He appeared to you."

Ellen closed her eyes. "Gallatin Roberts, if you are here, please speak to us. We come in peace to help, not harm. We are open to your message. Please use the energy from our devices to communicate with us. You can touch the REM-POD over there on the floor to make your presence known, if you're unable to manifest yourself to us."

One of the candles blew out as the image of the weeping man appeared and disappeared near the edge of the deck by the platform.

"Did you see that?" Sue whispered.

"Yes," the others said.

"Gallatin Roberts?" Ellen said. "Will you appear to me again? I'm ready to listen."

Nothing happened for several seconds.

"Why don't we try using the Ouija Board?" Tanya suggested. "Maybe he can speak to us that way."

Tanya and Ellen scooted their chairs closer to the bench, where Sue was sitting, and used their laps as a table for the board. Then they gingerly touched the planchette with the tips of their fingers as Sue pushed the device in a counterclockwise motion three times.

"Let's not forget to say goodbye," Sue whispered once she'd finished moving the planchette.

"Gallatin Roberts?" Ellen asked again, staring at the spot where he had momentarily appeared. "Are you here with us?"

The planchette moved to YES.

"Do you wish to tell us something?" Ellen asked.

The planchette moved to I and N. Then it circled around and stopped again on N before continuing to O-C-E-N-T.

"Innocent?" Tanya asked.

The planchette moved to YES.

Ellen cleared her throat. "Are you referring to the accusations made against you for misappropriating public funds to the bank just before it collapsed?"

The planchette circled the board and returned to YES.

"Can you prove your innocence?" Sue asked.

Again, the planchette circled the board and returned to YES.

Ellen lifted her brows and glanced at her friends. If the spirit could prove his innocence, then perhaps he could move on.

"How?" Tanya asked.

The planchette spelled M-Y.

"My," Tanya whispered.

"A-U-T-O-B-I-O-G-R-A-P-H-Y."

"You wrote an autobiography?" Ellen asked. "Where is it?"

Another candle flickered and went out, and a cold chill filled the air.

The planchette spelled out T-R-U-N-K.

"Trunk?" Tanya asked. "What trunk? Where is it?"

The planchette spelled B-A-S-E-M-E-N-T.

"Here, at Biltmore House?" Ellen wondered out loud.

The planchette slid to YES.

Tanya scratched her head. "I wonder why his trunk would be here."

The planchette began to move again. This time, it spelled G-R-A-N-D-D-A-U-G-H-T-E-R.

Tanya leaned forward. "Granddaughter?"

"Who's your granddaughter?" Sue asked.

The planchette spelled D-O-C-E-N-T.

"A docent here at Biltmore?" Tanya said.

The planchette moved to YES.

Sue lifted her brows. "What's her name?"

The planchette spelled out L-I-N-D-A.

"Linda what?" Ellen wanted to know.

The planchette spelled B-R-A-C-K-E-N.

Tanya sat up. "Wasn't Linda the name of our docent?"

"Gallatin, was your granddaughter our docent today?" Ellen asked.

The planchette didn't move.

"Is Linda in her early seventies?" Tanya asked.

The planchette circled around and returned to YES.

"I wonder why Gallatin is reaching out to us when he could have told Shiri," Ellen said with her head cocked to the side.

The planchette began to move again. It spelled I-G-N-O-R-E-S-M-E.

"What?" Sue furrowed her brows.

"Ignores me," Tanya said. "Does Shiri ignore you, Gallatin?"

The planchette moved to YES.

"We promise to find your granddaughter, Gallatin," Ellen said reassuringly. "We'll ask her to open your trunk and show us your autobiography. If you're right and it proves your innocence, then we'll take it to the proper authorities."

The planchette practically flew across the board as it quickly spelled E-X-O-N-E-R-A-T-E-M-E.

"He wants to be exonerated," Tanya said.

"We'll do our best," Sue promised.

The planchette spelled out N-O-W.

Ellen clicked her tongue. "He wants us to search for his trunk tonight?"

The planchette moved to YES.

"But this basement is huge," Tanya pointed out. "Where do we begin?"

Ellen opened her bag. "I have a pair of dousing rods in here. Should we give them a try?"

"We may as well," Sue said. "What have we got to lose?"

CHAPTER TWELVE

Gallatin Roberts

Tanya packed up the Ouija Board, and Sue collected the candles, as Ellen held the dousing rods—one in each hand—parallel to one another.

"Gallatin Roberts," Ellen said from the swimming pool deck. "Please use these dousing rods to lead us to the trunk containing your autobiography. Move the tips closer together if we are headed in the right direction. Move them further apart if we are going the wrong way."

"Oh, there she is," Marcia's voice carried across the empty pool from the doorway, where she stood beside her husband, Brian's brother, Mike. "Hey, Ellen, we're heading upstairs to bed and just wanted to say goodnight."

"What are you doing?" Mike asked. "Ghost hunting? On your son's wedding night?"

Ellen dropped her hands to her side and blushed. "Sort of." She set the rods down on one of the chairs and crossed the room to give her in-laws a hug. "Thanks so much for coming. It means a lot to Brian and to me."

"We wouldn't have missed it," Mike said. "It was good to see you ladies again."

Tanya and Sue gave them a wave.

"Goodnight," Mike said.

"Goodnight," Sue and Tanya said.

"See you in the morning for our champagne breakfast at the winery. Right?" Ellen asked.

"Right," Marcia said. "See you then."

Once they were alone again, Ellen took up the dousing rods and repeated her instructions to Gallatin Roberts. For several long seconds, nothing happened. Ellen decided to cross the room toward the gymnasium, where Mike and Marcia had just left. As she neared the doorway, the tips of the dousing rods moved toward one another.

"This way," she said to her friends.

Sue and Tanya followed as Ellen turned left, and the tips of the rods moved ever so slightly inward again. She followed a long corridor. As she came to the end of it, the rod tips crossed in front of a closed door.

"Does he want us to go in here?" Tanya wondered.

Ellen turned the doorknob and was pleasantly surprised when it opened. It was a small storage room filled with paintings, furniture, and knickknacks.

"They have a lot of storage in this house," Sue remarked.

Holding the dousing rods apart, Ellen said, "Gallatin, please direct us to your trunk."

Ellen walked past a wooden rocking chair, two end tables, a painted portrait, and a collection of vases to the corner of the room, where the rod tips crossed. In the corner of the room sat a wooden trunk about three feet wide, two feet high, and two feet deep.

"This is it," Ellen said.

"It's locked." Sue lifted the padlock, but it didn't budge. "How does he expect us to open it?"

Ellen and Tanya glanced around the room for something to use to break the lock. Then Ellen had the idea of inserting the tip of one of the dousing rods into the keyhole. After fiddling with it for a few minutes, her hands were pushed away by an invisible force. She jumped back in shock when the rod seemed to move of its own accord. Then it and the padlock fell to the floor.

The three friends stared in silence for a few seconds before Tanya said, "Thank you, Gallatin."

Shoving the dousing rods back into her bag, Ellen found her flashlight and turned it on as Sue lifted the lid of the trunk and released the scent of almonds and vanilla into the otherwise musty-smelling room. Among photographs, letters, scrapbooks, loose-leaf documents, and a key to the city of Asheville, were three leather-bound diaries.

"These diaries must contain his autobiography," Ellen whispered.

"Why don't we go someplace comfortable and read through them," Sue suggested. "But someplace away from the other wedding guests, so we're not caught snooping."

"How about the main kitchen?" Tanya said as she gathered the diaries. "We passed it on the way here. It's got a table we could sit at."

Ellen closed the lid to the trunk and stood upright. "Lead the way."

The main kitchen contained a large black iron oven and stove, black open cupboards for dishes, a long wooden island with a pot rack above it, and a small, wooden table for four.

Sue hesitated. "Wasn't the servants' dining room just down the hall? I think we should go down there. I don't trust the chairs in here."

Ellen and Tanya followed Sue to a room with a much larger table with eight wooden chairs on each side.

"Well, these chairs don't look much sturdier," Sue complained.

Ellen sat on one end of the table. "They've held up this long."

"That's not a compelling argument, in my opinion," Sue said as she tested one out.

"Now, *this* is *Downton Abbey*," Ellen said as she looked around the room. "I feel like we're on the television set."

"Which character are you?" Tanya asked as she gave each friend a diary. "I call Edith."

"Seriously?" Sue said. "She was the sister who was always passed up."

"But was the most independent, after Sybil," Tanya argued.

"I'd be Mary, hands down," Ellen said as she opened the diary Tanya had given her. "What about you, Sue?"

"Well, as much as I'd love to be Mary, or even her mother, I'd more likely be cast as one of the grandmothers."

"They're the best characters, anyway," Tanya said with a laugh.

"Well, if we're going by who we'd be cast as," Ellen said, "I suppose I'd choose Isobel Crawley. She's my favorite older character."

"Now, I didn't mean for anyone to agree with me," Sue pointed out with a look of mock reproach on her face. "You were supposed to say I'd make a perfect Mary."

"Of course, you would," Tanya said.

"Minus the sarcasm, please," Sue said.

Tanya chuckled as she sat beside Ellen, across from Sue. "Okay, should we each skim a journal and see if we can find what we need to exonerate Gallatin?"

"Let's do it," Ellen said.

Ellen began to read and was immediately taken in by the humble, honest voice of Gallatin as a young man. She read his story from 1895, just before entering Weaverville College, of travelling to Asheville in his uncle's wagon to use his last few dollars to buy a suit. He'd left his package in his uncle's wagon for a few minutes outside of the post office, only to return to find it stolen. He wrote about his feelings of helplessness, being away from home with no money to buy decent clothes. He decided to seek help from the police who caught the thief and asked Gallatin to testify against the crook at court. The trial lasted a week. According to Gallatin, it changed his life, for he knew then and there that he wanted to become a lawyer, just like the men in the courtroom.

Ellen skimmed through his descriptions of college life at various institutions, as he worked as a store clerk and then a schoolteacher. She also skimmed through his life at Wake Forest University, where he studied law, after which, he went into politics. She was fascinated by his honesty and self-criticism and found it hard to believe that he could be guilty of misappropriating millions of city funds.

"Here we go," Tanya said. "He talks about an argument he had with another city official over money that had gone missing. He accused his colleague of stealing it and swore he would find proof. I think this is it. This is what we need to exonerate him!"

"I wonder why Linda hasn't opened her grandfather's trunk," Sue said. "You'd think she'd be curious, especially as someone who's interested in history."

"Maybe she didn't have a key," Ellen offered.

"Still," Sue said. "I'd have found a way."

"Sue would have used her gun," Tanya teased.

The lights overhead flickered, and the lid to the Ouija Board, which was sitting on the table next to Tanya, popped open.

All three ladies jumped up in their seats.

"What was that?" Sue cried.

Ellen reached across the table and removed the board from its box. "Maybe Gallatin has something more to say to us."

The three friends placed their fingertips on the planchette.

Sue shook her head as she made a circular motion with the planchette on the board. "We didn't say goodbye after our last session. Let's be sure to do it this time."

"Gallatin Robert?" Ellen asked. "Are you there?"

The planchette moved to YES.

"Do you have something more to say to us?" Ellen asked.

The planchette circled the board again before spelling S-H-E.

"She?" Tanya read.

Then it spelled K-N-O-W-S.

"She knows," Tanya said.

Y-O-U.

"She knows you," Tanya said. "Maybe he means Linda, his grand-daughter."

"Because she was our docent," Sue speculated.

The planchette spelled A-R-E.

"Are," Tanya repeated.

H-E-R-E.

"Oh," Ellen said, understanding now. "He says that she knows we're here. Linda is expecting us, Gallatin?"

The planchette moved to NO.

Ellen glanced at her friends with a look of confusion, but before she could ask another question, the planchette spelled Z-E-L-D-A.

"Zelda knows we are here," Tanya said.

The planchette moved to YES before spelling B-E-W-A-R-E.

Tanya gasped, and Ellen's mouth dropped open.

"Who's Zelda?" Sue wondered.

"The only Zelda I've ever heard of is Zelda Fitzgerald," Ellen said. "The wife of the novelist."

The planchette circled the board and moved to YES. Then it spelled D-A-N-G-E-R.

The overhead light flickered and went out as the three ladies gaped at one another. There was enough light from the hall to see by.

"What kind of danger, Gallatin?" Tanya asked.

The planchette didn't move.

"Gallatin?" Ellen asked. "Are you there?"

The planchette didn't move.

"He's gone," Sue said. "What a way to make an exit."

Ellen was about to agree when suddenly she felt hands at her neck. She kicked and flailed against the invisible force, coughing against the pressure on her throat.

"Ellen?" Tanya asked. "What's wrong?"

Tears flooded Ellen's eyes as she struggled to breathe. Her heart raced, and she grunted against the pressure, trying to think despite the panic overwhelming her. Finally, she jumped up from her chair and ran down the hall to the main kitchen.

"Ellen?" Sue called from the corridor.

Ellen caught her breath and met her friends in the hall. "Something was choking me."

Tanya raised her brows. "Oh, my God. Let's get out of here."

CHAPTER THIRTEEN

Nighttime Antics

Ellen lay beside Brian in her silk, cheetah print pajamas on the edge of sleep in the glorious Louis XV room, feeling good about what she and her friends had discovered in the basement. She hoped to meet up with Gallatin's granddaughter, Linda, before leaving Asheville to discuss steps toward publishing the diaries and exonerating the past mayor of Asheville.

She also felt good about how the rest of the night had gone for Lane and Maya. The dance hadn't ended until eleven o'clock, and most of the guests had stayed until the very end to wish Lane and Maya a happy wedding night. The bride and groom had gotten so drunk that Ellen had worried they might not make it up the stairs.

Brian was fast asleep beside her on a full bed beneath an ivory and floral duvet. The large floral print was made of red velvet, and it was repeated in the wallpaper above ivory wainscoting and in the curtains flanking a bank of windows. Beside them were glass doors leading to a balcony that overlooked the front of the estate—the great lawn with its fountain and Christmas tree, the *rampe douce*, and the esplanade beyond. Opposite them was an ivory gilded fireplace—the centerpiece of the room. The fire in the hearth gave Ellen just enough light to see by.

An ivory damask daybed was situated in front of the windows to the balcony, and, in the corner, a wooden bassinet and chair were arranged before an armoire with cloth panels. The docent had said that the bassi-nette was used by Edith for Cornelia's crib and later by Cornelia for her baby sons, George Henry Vanderbilt Cecil and William Amherst Vanderbilt Cecil.

It had been a long, eventful day. It had been a beautiful, joyful day. It had been a day of powerful emotions. Ellen was exhausted, but not too exhausted to say a prayer asking that Lane and Maya's wedding day might serve as a prelude to what their married life would become—a time of prosperity and joy.

She had just drifted off when she felt a finger run along the bottom of her foot. Flinching, she pulled her knee up and opened her eyes. Brian lay fast asleep beside her. Supposing she had imagined it, she took a deep breath and tried again to go to sleep.

But now the finger ran across the bottom of her other foot. She froze as she felt the bed give to the weight of someone sitting on the edge of it beside her. Slowly, she held her breath and opened her eyes, only to find no one there. As she scanned the room for signs of a phantom, she saw the door to the balcony slowly open.

With her heart thumping against her ribs, Ellen picked up her thick flannel robe from the foot of the bed and put it on, along with a pair of fuzzy slippers, before stepping out onto the private balcony beneath the bright, full moon.

The ballerina appeared again beside Ellen as a full-bodied apparition. Up close, she was quite beautiful, with curly, gold hair that was as wild as the mountains and blue eyes that were as deep as the sky in the morning.

"I need the moon," she said. "I've been trying to lure you outside all night."

Ellen gawked, unable to speak.

"Snap out of it," the ghost said.

"I'm sorry," Ellen said. "Who are you? Why have you come to me?"

"My name is Zelda Fitzgerald."

Ellen gasped and backed toward the house. "Are-are you going to hurt me?"

Zelda's mouth opened wide, and a horrendous cackle rasped from her throat.

Terrified, Ellen rushed back inside and closed the balcony door behind her. Then she quickly found her way to the bed and crawled beneath the velvet duvet, clutching the *gris gris* at her chest.

But the hands circled around her throat, choking her. Unable to breathe, Ellen climbed from the bed and rushed to the bathroom. The spirit of Zelda lost its grip.

"Ellen?" Brian asked sleepily.

From the bathroom, she said, "Sorry to wake you. I'm alright."

Ellen studied herself in the bathroom mirror before splashing water on her face. She had to do something to stop the ghost from harassing her. After dabbing her face dry, she made her way to her phone on the bedside table and texted Sue and Tanya in their group text.

"Are you awake? I just saw Zelda. She's the ballerina."

She waited as three dots indicated Sue was typing.

"Yes." Sue wrote. "Want to meet?"

"Oh, my God!" Tanya typed. "What happened?"

"Meet me in the library?" Ellen wrote.

"Yes," Sue wrote again.

"See you there," Tanya typed.

Ellen grabbed her shoulder bag and carried it with her down the hall to the passage that led to the second-floor balcony of the library. As she descended the narrow, winding staircase, Tanya, wearing gray sweats and a sweatshirt, caught up with her.

"Are you okay?" she asked Ellen.

Ellen closed her fluffy robe more tightly around her. "Just shaken. She tried to choke me again."

"Wait, again?" Tanya asked. "What do you mean again?"

"I'm assuming it was her choking me in the servants' dining room. It wouldn't have been Gallatin."

"No, you're right."

Sue arrived not long after in her robe and slippers and followed them down the small staircase to the library below.

"Will this thing hold?" Sue asked as she descended.

"Only one way to find out," Tanya said.

Once they were safely on the first floor of the library, they sat on burgundy damask furniture before the black marble fireplace. There was nothing left of the fire but a bed of burning ash.

"Tell us what happened," Sue said as she sat on the sofa beside Ellen.

"She attacked me again," Ellen said. "We need to find out what she wants, so she'll stop trying to kill me."

"What if that's what she wants?" Sue said with a frown. "To kill you?"

"Then we need to find a way to banish her," Ellen said as a shudder crept down her back. "Did anyone bring any sage?"

Tanya and Sue shook their heads.

Ellen sighed. "Great. We'll have to make it through the night without it."

In that instant, a book fell from the second-story balcony to the bottom floor a few yards from their feet, startling them. Cautiously, Ellen got up from the couch and picked up the book.

"*The Great Gatsby*," she said, reading the title on the cover. The book had been bound in leather, as had most of the texts in the collection.

Just then, a second book fell from the balcony and hit Ellen on the head.

"Ow!" she cried, taking a step back.

"Are you okay?" Tanya asked, rushing to her side.

"Yeah, but that hurt." She rubbed her head to stop it from smarting.

Tanya picked up the book. "F. Scott Fitzgerald's *Tender Is the Night*."

Sue crossed the room to where Ellen and Tanya were standing. "I wonder if there might be a clue in those books."

Ellen combed through *The Great Gatsby* while Tanya did the same with *Tender Is the Night.*

"I don't see anything," Ellen said after a few minutes.

Just then, the black iron poker, which had been hanging on a stand beside the hearth alongside tongs, a broom, and a shovel, slowly lifted in the air with the pointed end directed at Tanya.

"What on earth?" Tanya muttered.

"Let's get out of here," Ellen said.

She and Tanya dropped the books and scurried to the door. Sue hurried after them. Ellen turned to see the poker standing up with the pointed end pierced through one of the books on the floor.

Sue caught up to Ellen and Tanya at the entrance to the tapestry gallery. "I don't know if she meant to impale me or her husband's book, but, thankfully, she did the latter."

Ellen heard voices. She held her arm out to stop Tanya and Sue from continuing into the tapestry room. "Shh. Someone's in there."

Standing in front of one of two fireplaces—the one closest to them—were Melissa Dresden and Ted Stone.

Ellen ducked behind a blue couch, even though it killed her knees. Tanya joined her. Sue, flurrying for a moment in a state of panic, skirted past them and hid behind a Christmas tree.

"I was about to go to bed," Melissa was saying. "James is waiting for me. What do you want?"

"This is going to sound crazy, but I had a dream about your sister tonight. I guess it was a dream, only I was awake."

Ellen covered her mouth and lifted her brows. Tanya mirrored Ellen's expression with her own.

"What do you mean?" Melissa said. "What happened?"

Ted sat on one of the blue couches closest to the fireplace. "I was getting dressed for bed when she appeared to me and said she was sorry. When I asked what she meant, she told me to talk to you."

"She spoke to you?" Melissa asked.

"Not for long. She disappeared soon after. I tried to go to bed but couldn't get what had happened out of my head. I'm glad I caught you before you turned in. Thanks for meeting me. Do you have any idea why your sister came to me to say she was sorry?"

Melissa sat on the opposite side of the sofa from Ted and covered her face with her hands. "Oh, Ted."

"Tell me," he said gently.

"I lied to you."

"Lied?"

"I did it because my sister loved you, too, and I couldn't bear to hurt her."

Ted stood up. "What?"

Melissa lowered her hands and looked up at him. "She had it bad for you. I was afraid we'd be miserable our whole lives if I went through with it. She'd be heartbroken, I'd feel guilty, and you'd be stuck in the middle."

Ted began to pace. "What exactly are you trying to say, Melissa? Are you saying that, even though you told me otherwise forty-five years ago, you loved me like a wife loves a husband?"

Melissa took a deep breath and slowly nodded.

Ted's face turned red, and, through gritted teeth, he said, "I can't believe you did that to me. I would have done anything for you, and you lied to me."

"Keep your voice down," she said.

"I've spent forty-six years feeling hurt and deceived by you. I thought you led me on only to break my heart. But this is worse. Much worse. It turns out you loved me but didn't trust me enough with the truth. And all these years I've had to take James's jabs."

Melissa climbed to her feet. "I did it for Melinda, Ted. I was trying to spare her the embarrassment. How was I to know that the second you didn't show up to the altar she'd run straight to you and confess her feelings?"

"You could have told me then," he said as tears streamed down his cheeks. "After she died. Forty-six years ago."

Melissa turned her back to Ted and stared at the diminishing fire in the hearth. "She died because you rejected her. I hated you for that."

"What was I supposed to do, Melissa? I loved *you*!"

Melissa shook her head and sobbed into her hands.

Ted heaved a heavy sigh and left the room through the main hall. Ellen could hear his angry steps as he ascended the grand spiral staircase.

Ellen whispered, "Should we do anything?"

Tanya shook her head. Together they waited another five minutes or so, until Melissa finally left the tapestry gallery. They listened as she crossed the main hall and headed upstairs.

"That was close," Sue said, emerging from behind the tree. "I was almost certain that Ted saw me."

"I was hoping for a happier ending for them," Tanya said, climbing to her feet.

Ellen grabbed Tanya's hand for help up. "Me, too."

"You'd think Ted would be happy to know that Melissa really loved him," Tanya said.

"He was hurt that she wasn't honest with him," Ellen said. "And I can understand that. Melissa should have told him the truth."

"She was trying to spare her sister embarrassment," Tanya argued.

Ellen shrugged. "Apparently, her sister didn't deserve it."

"But how was Melissa to know what her sister would do?" Tanya pointed out.

That's when Ellen noticed that Sue had grown very quiet and still.

"Sue? You okay?"

She pointed.

Ellen and Tanya followed her finger to the loggia off the gallery. Standing there bathed in moonlight was the figure of Zelda Fitzgerald in her pink tutu beckoning to them.

C H A P T E R   F O U R T E E N

Madness in the Moonlight

It was cold on the loggia, and the moon was bright. The Blue Ridge Mountains stood silent in the distance like useless sentinels.

Ellen, Sue, and Tanya huddled close together near the terrace door, ready to sprint back inside if the apparition threatened them.

With wide eyes, Ellen gazed at the full-bodied apparition. She looked as real in the moonlight as Tanya or Sue.

"I am not the wife of author F. Scott Fitzgerald."

Ellen pulled her robe more tightly around her. It was cold, but at least it was no longer snowing. "Who are you then?"

"Zelda Fitzgerald—an author in my own right. I would never want to be known as a famous person's wife."

Ellen glanced warily at her friends, wondering what harm this little pink spirit had in store for them. "Oh, I see."

"My mother was a writer. Did you know that?"

The three friends shook their heads.

"A writer and an artist, just like me. Her poems and sketches were published in newspapers."

"You must have been proud of her," Ellen said.

"She was also an actress and a singer and would have gone on to have a career in the opera or on the stage if she hadn't married my father, the judge. Men can ruin women's lives. Scott ruined mine."

Tanya, who was shivering, asked, "How so?"

The petite ballerina laid one hand on the stone rail of the terrace, put her heels together, and performed a plié. "I miss my mother. When I was a child, I knew nothing of doubt and insecurity. I went everywhere by myself, even in the poor districts." She dipped into another plié. "I climbed trees, played sports, walked on rooftops. There were no limits to my freedoms, to my achievements."

"How nice for you," Sue said with a hint of sarcasm.

"But I started dancing too late. I could have been great if I'd started young. That's what Madame Egorova said."

Ellen wanted to go inside. As thrilled as she was to be seeing this full-bodied apparition, she was also terrified and wished the ghost would get to the point. "I suppose we all have regrets."

"My greatest regret is not standing up to Scott about my writing. He stole my words. Did you know that?"

Once again, the three friends shook their heads.

"I drew Gatsby, so Scott could *see* him. I came up with the title, too. He wanted *Gold-Hatted Gatsby*. Isn't that awful? His second choice was *The High Bouncing Lover*. I was writing *Tender Is the Night* at the same time Scott was. My novel, *Save me the Waltz*, is essentially the same material. He made me delete the parts that he wanted in his book and then put me away so he could publish his book first."

Tanya arched a brow. "What do you mean he put you away?"

"He checked me into a sanitarium against my will. I wasn't allowed to write, so I took up dancing again. I poured my heart and soul into it. I was good, but I could never be great."

Sue rolled her eyes. "I'm sorry to hear that."

Ellen wished Sue would cut it with the sarcasm. Zelda might turn on them at any moment.

The ghost of Zelda lifted her leg and pointed her toe in the air. She swept it back to the floor and repeated the kick. "I could have been a great writer, though. Scott owes much of his fame and fortune to me, and no one knows it. So many of *my* words were used in Scott's stories and books."

Ellen crossed her arms. "Can you prove it?"

"Only if my letters and diaries have survived the ravages of time."

"Is this where you died, at the Biltmore?" Tanya asked.

"No, I died at a sanitarium not far from here," she said as she continued her ballet exercises. "I'd been sedated and locked in my room and was awaiting electroshock therapy when a fire spread and killed me in my sleep."

"How horrible," Tanya said through chattering lips.

"It took me awhile to figure out that I was dead. It took me even longer to piece together what had happened. I sometimes think the fire might have been started deliberately, but I have no proof."

"Who would have done it?" Sue asked.

"Someone wishing to diminish me."

"Where would we find your letters?" Ellen asked.

Zelda lifted her leg back behind her and leaned forward with one arm stretched out. "I don't know."

Ellen gnawed on her bottom lip. What did this phantom want from them?

Zelda turned to hold the railing with the opposite hand and repeated the pointed kick with her other leg. "When I was young, I thought Scott would save me from my stifling father and the suffocating town of Montgomery."

"You grew up in Montgomery, Alabama?" Tanya asked.

"Yes, unfortunately. It was too small for me. Scott stood out from the crowd just as I did. He was my match in all ways. We walked on water together. He named the Jazz Age, for Heaven's sake, and made me the first flapper. I remember those early days when we talked about poetry on my front porch and he told me that according to Keats and Browning, he should marry me."

Hoping to keep her calm, Ellen said, "How romantic."

Zelda switched sides on the railing and resumed her pliés with her feet spread apart. "After he was discharged from the army, we snuck away together every chance we had. He was fascinated with my diary. That's when it all began. He took pages and pages of my diary and put them into *This Side of Paradise*, his first big hit. I never saw that diary again."

"Why didn't you stop him?" Sue asked.

"I wanted him to succeed. I wanted him to hit it big. I wanted to help. I didn't know at the time how big a sacrifice he would expect of me. We were happy then. We wanted to conquer New York together—and then the world. Instead, he conquered me."

"I still don't understand what you want from us," Sue said.

"I once wrote to him in a letter that we should die when we're thirty."

"Why would you say such a thing?" Tanya asked.

"I didn't want him to see me become old and ugly. You see, I was sure he would grow to be a handsome old man."

Sue frowned.

Fearing Sue was about to mock the ghost again, Ellen said, "I'm sorry you felt that way."

"I wish we would have died young together."

"You don't mean that," Tanya said.

"You don't know anything about it," Zelda said. Then, as she slid her right foot forward and made another plié, she added, "But even then, our long talks in those early days were mostly monologues. We took turns making speeches but neither of us really listened to the other or responded in any meaningful way."

Ellen shrugged. "I'm sure that's true of many couples."

"I learned rather quickly that Scott was afraid. He wrote to escape. He drank to escape. But I wasn't afraid, you see? I wanted to do things."

"What things?" Sue asked.

"Go to parties, visit New York, travel abroad, see the sites, *be* the sites. When I drank, it was to enhance what I was doing, not to escape it altogether. But the more he tried to escape, the more uncertain I became. He took my confidence away from me. I needed to be a spectacle, and he made that less and less possible for me. He's the reason people thought me mad—I even thought myself mad. Maybe I was. Maybe I lost my mind. I needed to be seen. I'd grown invisible."

Ellen was reminded of the Pink Lady at the Grove Park Inn. Like the young mistress, Zelda wanted to be observed. She wanted to be on display but had been overshadowed by her husband.

"I tried to die young. I overdosed on sleeping pills, but Sara made me drink olive oil and saved my life."

"Sara?" Tanya asked.

"Sara Murphy. She was my friend."

Then, as she brought her right foot in front of her left, the ballerina said, "Did you know that several of my stories were published under Scott's name, even though they were one hundred percent mine? Others were published with both of our names, even though Scott hadn't contributed a single thing to them. Why is that, do you suppose?"

"Maybe the publisher thought they would earn more money with Scott's name on them?" Tanya offered.

"Yes, but Scott should have stuck up for me. Instead, when I wanted to write, he forced me into a sanitarium. The rest cure only made me worse. I needed to dance, to paint, to hike—anything but lie there day after day beneath those horrendous bandages, my head and neck on fire from eczema. And I was on bromides and morphine and other useless remedies that did nothing for me. I begged Scott to let me come home, but my doctor said that if Scott kept drinking, he would continually trigger me into madness. I think I drove Scott to drink, and he drove me to madness. We ruined each other because we couldn't love each other like we had in the beginning."

"The rest cure?" Sue asked. She turned to Ellen. "Like the Gold House?"

Ellen gnawed on her lower lip recalling what they'd learned about the Greek Revival in the King William District of San Antonio, where their adventures into the paranormal first began.

"How can we help you to move on?" Tanya asked Zelda.

Zelda stopped her ballet exercises and stood erect. "Move on? I don't want to move anywhere. I told you, I want to be a spectacle. I need to be seen. But I also need to be credited for my work, and you must do that for me, or I'll kill someone this very night. When I was young, during a party thrown by Isadora Duncan, I threw myself down the stairs because I felt obliterated by the attention Isadora was giving to my husband. I hadn't cared whether I lived or died. I just wanted to be noticed, don't you see? And tonight, I will push someone down the stairs if you don't get me the credit that I deserve. One of your loved ones will become a fellow ghost of Biltmore House."

That horrendous cackle that had frightened Ellen earlier in the night escaped from Zelda's throat and sent a chill down her spine. Then the phantom grew in height and lifted her hands, like the claws of an old witch.

Fearing the hands would resume their hold on her throat, Ellen scrambled to the balcony door. Her friends quickly followed. They raced to the couch in the tapestry gallery where Ted Stone and Melissa Dresden had been sitting moments before.

As they caught their breath and warmed themselves by the fire, Ellen pulled a shaker of salt from her purse and sprinkled a circle of protection around them.

"What? Here?" Sue asked.

"Just for now, so we can think," Ellen explained. "I don't want her choking me again."

"What are we going to do?" Tanya said, her face as white as the specter's had been. "It's the middle of the night. What does she expect us to do?"

Sue glanced at her phone. "It's nearly midnight."

"This is crazy," Ellen agreed. "Do you think she's really capable of killing someone?"

"I don't want to find out," Tanya said.

"We need to think," Ellen said.

"I personally think she's crazy," Sue said. "I say we banish her."

"But we don't have any sage," Ellen pointed out.

Tanya took out her phone. "Let's search for other methods. There's bound to be something we can try."

"I wish Shiri were still here," Sue said as she scrolled through her search results. "I bet she knows one or two."

"Do you think Zelda's telling the truth about her husband plagiarizing her words?" Ellen asked.

Sue lifted a finger. "Listen to this, there's a series about her on Amazon Prime!"

"What?" Ellen sat up straight. "I've never heard of it. Have you?"

"Apparently, it didn't do very well," Sue said. "It was first aired in 2017 and flopped, so they didn't make a second season."

Tanya leaned forward. "That's why we haven't heard of it."

Sue lifted her finger again. "Hold on. This website talks about Scott's plagiarism of Zelda!"

"Seriously?" Ellen took Sue's phone and skimmed through the article. "You're right. Maybe if we read this out loud, she'll hear us and leave us alone."

"It's worth a shot," Sue said, taking back her phone. "Should we summon her?"

"What makes you think she left?" Ellen wondered.

"I think we're better off banishing her," Tanya said. "Why risk it? She's threatening the lives of your loved ones. And I found something that may do the trick."

Tanya read them the directions of a banishing spell involving salt, fire, and a link to the person to be banished.

"How will you pull that off without something that once belonged to Zelda?" Sue asked.

"We can use the book she impaled earlier," Ellen pointed out.

"That's what I was thinking," Tanya said. "Want to get it?"

"I'm not sure about leaving this circle," Sue said. "You want to risk it?"

Tanya scratched her chin. "We can't stay here all night. I'll just run over and grab it right quick."

Ellen and Sue watched as Tanya jumped up and sprinted from the gallery to the library. Tanya was dashing back with the fire poker and the impaled book on the end flapping like a bird, when she suddenly stopped short, dropped the poker and the book along with it, and clutched her throat.

Ellen jumped to her feet. "Tanya?"

Tanya's face turned white as she hacked and fell to her knees.

"Tanya!" Sue cried.

Ellen and Sue left the circle of protection and helped Tanya to her feet. Ellen picked up the poker with the book and helped Sue to half-drag Tanya back to the circle. After they'd entered the circle, Tanya fell back on the sofa, finally able to breathe.

"That woman is evil," Tanya said when she could speak. "The sooner we banish her, the better."

Sue pulled the book from the end of the poker and handed it to Tanya.

"Oh, Ellen, you do it." Tanya passed the book to Ellen. "I'm still recovering."

Ellen wasn't sure what to do. "Okay." She held the book with both hands and closed her eyes. "I call upon the elements of earth and fire to help me bind the ghost of Zelda Fitzgerald to this book."

A horrendous shriek cried out from the loggia outside.

Ellen opened her eyes. "What did you say to do next, Tanya?"

"Throw it in the fire, and then, when it's nothing but ash, you pour salt on it as you say words to banish her from Biltmore."

"You think I can throw it into the fire from here, without leaving the circle?" Ellen climbed to her feet and stood just inside the salt barrier.

In that moment, a scream sounded from the grand spiral staircase. To Ellen, it sounded like Maya.

CHAPTER FIFTEEN

Christmas Carols

Ellen scrambled from the tapestry gallery, through the main hall, to the grand spiral staircase and looked up to see Lane holding Maya in his arms on the third-floor balcony.

"Lane?" Ellen called in a voice loud enough to be heard by the new-lyweds but not too loud as to wake up the other guests. "Everything okay?"

Lane smiled at her from over the balcony rail and waved. Then he took Maya's hand and the two of them, wearing their matching flannel robes and fuzzy socks, started down the stairs.

"What are they doing?" Sue asked, once she'd caught up to Ellen and Tanya at the base of the staircase.

"They're coming down." Ellen ascended the steps. "I wonder what they're doing up at this hour."

"Maybe they were too excited to sleep," Tanya said, following.

"I don't want that evil ghost getting anywhere near them, Tanya. We must protect them. I'm scared to death."

Ellen glanced back to see Sue standing at the base of the stairs wear-ing a look of indecision.

"I'll come back down in a minute, Sue," she said. "Just wait there."

"But I'm afraid to stay here alone."

"Go back to the circle," Tanya said.

"But if something happens to me before I make it, you won't know until it's too late. I'll just wait here."

Ellen hurried up toward the second floor to meet Lane and Maya. "What are you two doing up?"

"I could ask the same of you," Lane said. "But I think I already know the answer."

"I wish you'd go back to your room," Ellen said. She wanted to add, "Where it's safe," but she didn't want to worry the newlyweds on their special night.

"Lane promised to play me Christmas carols on the Biltmore piano," Maya said with a gleam in her eyes. "I brought my phone to capture it on video."

"Aren't you afraid of waking up the other guests?" Ellen asked.

"I'll play softly," Lane said as he and Maya stepped past her and Tanya and continued down the stairs toward the main floor.

"Merry Christmas, by the way," Maya added. "I want to remember this day forever."

"Merry Christmas," Ellen said as she and Tanya followed them down.

"Merry Christmas," Tanya said.

Then Maya stumbled and fell into Lane's arms again. Ellen and Tanya shrieked.

"Mom, it's okay. I got her."

"That's the second time you pushed me," Maya said.

"Stop. I didn't push you. You lost your step."

"I did not," Maya insisted. "I felt you push me on the balcony. I could have died."

Ellen shot Tanya a worried look.

"You're still drunk," Lane said.

"I'm not drunk."

"There, there," Sue said as they neared the foot of the stairs. "It's bad luck to bicker on your wedding night."

"And on Christmas morning to boot," Ellen said.

Sue arched a brow at Ellen. "Aren't you going to warn them about the—"

Ellen shook her head and motioned to Sue to zip her mouth shut. She didn't want to spoil things for Lane and Maya when there was a chance that Zelda could be contained.

"Warn us about what?" Lane asked.

"Oh, it's nothing," Ellen said. "One of the toilets down the hall isn't working, so I'd avoid using that one if I were you."

"For sure," Maya said, leading Lane by the hand.

As the newlyweds headed for the music room, Ellen hung back near the foot of the stairs with Sue and Tanya.

"This is what we're going to do," Ellen said. "We'll very discreetly create a circle of protection around them at the piano. Then we'll go back to banishing Zelda. Hopefully we can get this done without another hitch."

Ellen rushed back to the tapestry gallery to grab her bag, and then caught up to Sue and Tanya as they entered the music room, where they found Alison and Luke still in their wedding clothes sitting together on a wooden loveseat near the piano. Luke's lips were smeared with Alison's lipstick.

Ellen and Sue exchanged looks of surprise.

"That shade of lipstick looks good on you, Luke," Sue teased.

Under her breath, Ellen said, "Don't embarrass them." Aloud, she said, "Merry Christmas, you two. You're up late."

"Merry Christmas, Mama." Alison stood up and gave Ellen a hug. She reeked of alcohol.

"Lane's going to play us some Christmas carols," Maya said as Lane sat in the chair at the piano.

"But not too loudly," Ellen said. "We don't want to wake up the others."

Lane cracked his knuckles, put his fingers on the keys, and started playing *Jingle Bells*. Maya stood near him with her phone pointed at him.

As they softly sang along, Ellen snuck the saltshaker from her bag and carefully walked around, pretending to dance along, as she sprinkled the salt onto the wooden floor, making sure all four of the young people were well within the boundaries. Her children were used to her dramatic ways, so they didn't seem to suspect that anything out of the ordinary was happening.

With the circle made and the carol ended, Ellen said, "You kids stay here. We'll be right back."

"Where are you going, Mama?" Alison asked with hooded eyes.

"Uh, to the restroom. But stay here. Don't leave until we come back. Promise?"

"You got it," Alison said with a smile.

"Don't forget about the broken toilet," Maya warned.

"Of course," Ellen said, feeling the blood rush to her cheeks.

Lane started another carol—*We Wish You a Merry Christmas*—as Ellen and her friends hurried back to their task of banishing the evil spirit.

When they reached their circle of protection in the tapestry gallery, the impaled book, *Tender Is the Night*, was gone.

"Where did it go?" Tanya said, glancing around.

Ellen looked beneath the furniture. The poker was there, but there was no sign of the book.

"She took it, I bet," Sue said. "We'll have to get the other one—*The Great Gatsby*."

"I'll go," Ellen said. "You two wait here."

"Are you sure?" Tanya asked with a frown.

"What choice do we have?" Ellen said irritably. Then she added, "I'm sorry. I'm just scared, that's all."

"I'll go with you," Tanya said. "Just in case."

They scurried across the tapestry gallery to the library, where the fire had completely died. They searched the floor for *The Great Gatsby*, but as with the other book, it had vanished.

Ellen frantically looked beneath the furniture. "I don't see it. Do you?"

When Tanya made no reply, Ellen stopped searching and glanced over at her friend. Tanya was standing as still as a statue and appeared to be holding her breath.

"Tanya?"

Ellen followed Tanya's gaze to the second-floor balcony where the ghost in the tan cardigan and navy trousers stood peering down at them.

"Hello," he said. "I'm George, and this is my home."

Ellen couldn't speak. She gawked at the full-bodied apparition as a chill crept down her spine and goosebumps crawled up her arms.

"You really shouldn't give up on her, you know," he said. "Zelda deserves peace as much as anyone."

"W-what about you?" Tanya asked. "Don't you want to find peace?"

"I already have," he said. "This place is my little piece of heaven. Why would I ever leave it?"

"She threatened my family," Ellen said. "My friends."

"It's your choice," he said. "I'm sure the others would be glad to be rid of her either way."

"There are others?" Tanya asked through quivering lips.

He gave her a nod and disappeared.

Ellen stood speechless for several seconds.

Tanya snapped her back to reality. "What do we do?"

"Let's get back to the circle of protection and see what Sue says."

They hurried from the library to Sue's side in the tapestry room and told their friend what had happened.

"If we can help a Shinigami to find redemption, surely we can help Zelda Fitzgerald," Sue said, referring to their case in Santa Fe.

"What if we summon her and prove to her that others know about Scott's plagiarism," Tanya said. "Do you think she'd want to cross over?"

Ellen shrugged. "I suppose it's worth a try. But let's hurry before our carolers in the other room head up the stairs and put themselves in danger." Then she added, "She can only speak to us beneath the full moon. Should we return to the loggia?"

Sue sighed. "I suppose so. Let's take the salt."

They hurried onto the terrace, where the bright moon illuminated the snow-covered landscape behind the estate. At the end of the loggia, where Melissa Dresden had been standing earlier that evening, the ghost of Zelda appeared on tiptoe with her arms stretched gracefully overhead.

"I should have killed you," she said without a hint of anger. "I heard what you planned to do."

"We found an article about Scott's plagiarism," Sue said, taking out her phone. "There was even a television show made about you."

The ballerina's face lit up. "Really?"

Thankfully, Sue didn't add that the show was a flop.

"Please let us help you find peace," Tanya said. "Don't you want to cross over and be with your family?"

"I suppose I *would* like to see Scottie and my mom," she said. "Maybe my sisters, too."

"So, you've forgiven him, then?" Ellen asked.

"Who?"

"Scottie—Scott," Ellen said.

"Scottie is our daughter," she said. "I hope Scott's in hell."

"You don't mean that," Ellen said.

Zelda narrowed her eyes and hissed. Ellen and her friends took several steps back, toward the balcony door.

"Please, we have proof," Sue said.

"Have you seen the television show?" Zelda asked.

Ellen and her friends shook their heads.

"Then you don't know if my secret was made known to the viewing public. You have no idea."

"But the article," Sue insisted.

"One article isn't enough. I need to be exonerated!"

She reminded Ellen of Gallatin Roberts.

"Sue's blog," Tanya said suddenly. "It gets hundreds of hits a day."

"That's right!" Ellen cried, feeling hopeful. "Sue can write the truth on her blog, and thousands of people will read it."

"What's a blog?" Zelda asked with her nose upturned.

"It's an electronic diary that can be viewed by hundreds of thousands of people from their phones, laptops, and personal computers," Ellen explained. "Sue's blog is very popular."

"I want to see you do it," Zelda insisted.

Sue was chewing on a fingernail. "I didn't bring my laptop."

"Use your phone," Tanya said.

Ellen raised her hands in the air. "There was a computer downstairs, remember?"

"You mean in the room with the door that said *Authorized Personnel Only*?" Sue asked.

Ellen nodded. "But the door was wide open. Let's go."

"I want Zelda to promise that she'll leave our children alone," Sue said.

Zelda floated across the snow-covered terrace and hovered within inches of Sue's face. Sue stood frozen, unable to move or speak.

Ellen may have peed a little.

"Fine," Zelda said before she disappeared.

CHAPTER SIXTEEN

Authorized Personnel Only

Let's take the service elevator," Sue insisted, as they entered the tapestry room from the loggia, where they heard the kids singing to Lane's piano rendition of *Rudolph the Red-Nosed Reindeer.* "To avoid the labyrinthian storage rooms."

"Should we check on the kids first?" Ellen wondered. "We should remind them to stay put."

"It will only take a second," Tanya pointed out.

The three friends entered the music room. Tanya's son Mike and his partner, Seth, had joined the group, still wearing their tuxedos, but they weren't standing in the barely perceptible circle of protection. Mike was sitting near the fireplace, and Seth was warming himself at the hearth.

When they finished their song, Ellen said, "That's the Christmas spirit! Will you sing another? We'll be right back to join in."

"Where are you going now, Mama?" Alison, who had her hand in Luke's, asked.

"Er," Ellen looked to her friends for help.

"To get snacks," Sue said. "I have some up in my room. We'll be right back. Don't move."

"Good," Luke said. "I'm starving."

Tanya took Mike's hand and led him closer to the piano.

"What are you doing, Mom?"

"I want to snap a photo. Come on, Seth. Move in closer."

"Oh, Mom," Mike complained.

"It's okay," Seth said. "It'll be a great memory to have."

As she took the photo, Tanya added, "Don't move. We'll be right back."

Ellen led the way past the salon and breakfast room, past the banquet hall and butler's pantry, to the service elevator.

"Let's make this quick," Ellen said as she entered and pressed the button.

The very slow descent filled with whirs and knocks seemed to take forever. When the elevator finally came to a halt, Ellen pulled the door open, and they stepped into the corridor.

"This way," Tanya said, taking the lead. "It's just past the boiler room, remember?"

"Oh, thank God," Sue said. "My feet can't take much more."

"Hello?" a man's voice called from somewhere behind them. "No one's supposed to be down here."

"Oh no," Ellen whispered. "It's the Minotaur. Hide!"

"In here." Tanya led them into the boiler room.

They hurried past a huge boiler and into a smaller room with a duct hanging overhead, stacks of empty pallets to one side, and a few barrels stashed in one corner.

"Over here," Tanya whispered.

The young man seemed to be just outside the boiler room when he said, "If someone's down here, you need to return upstairs. This floor is off limits."

Ellen and her friends ducked behind the barrels. Sue was on her knees and wincing.

"Are you okay?" Ellen whispered.

She nodded but had obviously hurt herself.

"Hello?" the man called again. "I know I heard someone exit the service elevator. You need to come out and return upstairs."

"He's not going away," Tanya whispered. "What do we do?"

"Stay put," Sue said, still frowning. "It's all we can do." Then she added, "And pray. We can do that, too."

Ellen said a prayer, hoping the Minotaur would give up and go back to wherever he'd come from.

But her prayers went unanswered, for he was moving in on them, his footsteps just outside the room.

"Hello? I know someone's down—"

His voice was cut short by a hacking sound.

Ellen pressed her brows together and cupped her hand around one ear, hoping to get a better listen on what was happening. A full minute passed when they heard a thud. It sounded like the Minotaur had fallen.

"What was that?" Tanya whispered. "Should we check on him?"

"It could be a trap," Sue said. "Just wait."

Ellen climbed to her feet. "He could be hurt. I'm going to check."

Ellen tip-toed to the door of the room and peered into the boiler room. A heavy-set security guard in a white uniform with a badge on his shirt sat slumped against the wall with his legs sprawled out and his eyes closed. The poor thing couldn't be more than thirty years old.

Tanya came up behind her. "Oh, my God. Is he dead?"

Ellen bent over him, but before she could check for a pulse, Sue cried, "Don't touch him!"

Looking up at the hobbling Sue, Ellen asked, "Why not?"

"If he's dead, we don't want your DNA on him, do we?"

Tanya clapped her hands in front of the man's face, trying to stir him to, but the security guard didn't move.

"Oh, my God," Tanya said again.

A cold chill worked down the back of Ellen's neck. "Do you think Zelda did this?"

Limping from the boiler room, Sue said, "Let's just get on the computer and get out of here before anything else goes wrong."

"Let us help you," Tanya said as she draped Sue's arm on her shoulder and placed a hand on Sue's lower back. "Did you hurt yourself?"

"I fell down hard on my knees," she said. "I may have shattered my left kneecap. The pain is excruciating."

Ellen put Sue's other arm around her neck. "I'm so sorry. We need to get some ice on it, then."

"First the blog," Sue said. "Before someone else gets killed."

"You didn't have to do that, Zelda," Ellen said, not sure if the ghost was listening. "We would have figured out a way."

Once they were inside the office with the *Authorized Personnel Only* sign on the door, Tanya and Ellen helped Sue into the desk chair. Then Sue tried to log on.

"Great," Sue said. "The computer is password protected."

"Try *Biltmore*," Ellen suggested.

When it failed, Ellen said, "What about *Cordelia*?"

Another error message hit the screen.

"We're going to get locked out," Sue said. "Maybe Zelda knows the password."

"If not, there might be another ghost who does," Tanya pointed out.

"We left the Ouija Board upstairs," Ellen said with a sigh. "I could run up and get it."

"Tanya should go," Sue said. "She's faster."

"What if the security guard wakes up?" Tanya wanted to know.

"I hope he does," Ellen said, "but, unfortunately, I don't think he will be waking up, ever."

Sue shook her head. "He looked pretty dead to me."

"Okay, I'll do it. I'll be right back."

"Be careful," Ellen said.

Tanya gave her a weak smile before rushing from the room.

Ellen crouched near Sue. "Let me take a look at your knees."

Sue's left knee had swelled to the size of a cantaloupe.

"That doesn't look too good."

Sue pulled her robe over her legs. "Thanks for the diagnosis, doctor."

"Should we take you to the emergency room?"

"It's nearly one in the morning on Christmas day," Sue said. "How will we get there? We have no car and no shuttle. And I don't want to call for an ambulance. I can make it through the night."

"We should at least have Nolan take a look and see what he says."

"Don't wake him. He's got his hands full with Bri. He can look at it in the morning."

"I wish we had access to ice," Ellen said. "This isn't a hotel with an ice and vending room. I didn't even see a fridge in the main kitchen."

"Don't worry about it. I'll be fine."

"Was it the left foot that was shot in the case of the abandoned warehouse?" Ellen asked.

"No. It was the other one."

Ellen sighed, hoping Sue would be alright. She said a prayer asking that Sue wouldn't end up in a wheelchair after this. While she was at it, she prayed for Tanya's safe and quick return and for the safety of their kids.

"Ow," Sue said. "Something scratched me on the back of my neck."

Ellen lifted Sue's brown hair and turned down the collar of her robe to find a red mark beneath the thin leather cord on which she wore her *gris gris*.

"Have you been scratching yourself back here?" Ellen asked.

"No. But I swear I felt something sharp back there just now."

"You have a red mark." Then Ellen added, "We're working on it, Zelda. Leave us alone, or I swear, we'll banish you."

"I don't know if threatening her is the right approach," Sue said.

"She's making me angry."

"I have an idea," Sue said. "Remember how in Tulsa Miss Mabel used herself as a medium to draw what the spirits willed her to draw? And you did the same thing in Boulder City."

"So?"

"Tanya's taking forever. While we're waiting on her, why don't you try using this pen and paper. Maybe the spirits will help you write out the password."

"I suppose it's worth a try."

Ellen took the pen and notepad and closed her eyes. "Spirits of the other realm, we come in peace and mean no harm. We're trying to help the ghost of Zelda Fitzgerald to find peace, but to do that, we need the password to log onto this computer. If anyone here knows the password, please use the energy from the lights overhead to work through me and help me to write it out."

Keeping her eyes closed, Ellen bent over the desk and held the tip of the pen to the paper and waited. The house was far from quiet. It creaked and moaned and clattered with alarming regularity. Ellen could hear Sue close to her, panting. There was also the smell of cinnamon coffee nearby. Perhaps it had belonged to the poor security guard. Ellen was about to give up when she felt a strange pressure on her hand, and her mind went blank.

A moment later, Sue was shouting near her ear. "Ellen? Ellen, snap out of it!"

Feeling dazed and disoriented, she opened her eyes and looked around. "What happened?"

"Look."

Ellen followed Sue's gaze to the notepad, where words written in Ellen's hand read *Save yourselves.*

"Oh, hell," Ellen murmured as the hair on the back of her neck tingled. "That's not helpful at all."

"Yeah. I don't think that's the password."

Just then, they heard footsteps approaching. Ellen poked her head into the hall to see who was coming and sighed with relief to see Tanya carrying the box with the Ouija Board.

"I don't know how much good this is going to do," Ellen said before filling Tanya in on what had just transpired. "But let's give it a shot."

"We better, after what I just went through. The kids saw me running, and I told them this whole story about Sue falling, and… never mind. Let's do this."

Tanya removed the board from the box and set it on the desk in front of Sue.

"Oh, no, Sue," Tanya said, noticing her swollen knee. "You need a doctor."

"I'll be alright. Come on, let's get this over with."

Ellen and Tanya leaned over the desk with their fingers on the planchette beside Sue's.

"I'll lead," Sue said. "It helps distract me from the pain."

"Of course," Ellen said. "Go for it."

"Spirits of the other realm," Sue began. "We come in peace and mean no harm. We are seeking help in logging on to this computer. I know many of you were alive during a time when computers weren't yet in existence, but some of you must be familiar with them. And, even if you aren't, have you ever looked over the shoulder of someone logging onto this device? If so, did you ever notice a series of characters they had to enter before they could proceed? If you have witnessed this, and if you recall those characters, please spell them out for us using this Ouija Board."

Ellen just realized there weren't special characters, like ampersands, asterisks, and pound signs, on the Ouija Board. Were she and her friends wasting their time?

Nothing happened for a full minute, but then the planchette began to move. It spelled S-A-V-E-Y-O-U-R-S-E-L-V-E-S.

<u>CHAPTER SEVENTEEN</u>

Elevator Trouble

With no help from the spirits, Sue attempted to log on five more times before she was locked out of the computer in the room with *Authorized Personnel Only* on the door.

"Now what?" she asked.

"Try your phone," Ellen said. "I know it's not easy to text out an article, but what else can we do?"

Sue pulled her phone from her crossbody bag and, after tapping it a few times, said, "There's no service down here. We need to go upstairs."

"Great," Tanya said with a sigh.

"Zelda?" Ellen said. "We aren't giving up, okay? We're just going upstairs to use Sue's phone to post the article on the internet. I promise you that thousands of people will see this post before long. Trust us, okay?"

"Let me help you to your feet." Tanya offered Sue her shoulder.

Ellen tucked the Ouija Board into her shoulder bag and then helped Sue on the side opposite Tanya.

Sue winced.

"Try not to put any pressure on it," Ellen said.

"Easier said than done," Sue complained.

Very slowly, they made their way past the boiler room, where the security guard still slumped against the wall, to the service elevator.

"We should take you up to your room," Ellen said. "Can't you write your post from your bed? You need to stay off this foot."

"I don't want to leave the kids," she said. "Let's get them to safety first."

When they reached the main floor, Tanya said, "You wait here, Sue. We'll get the kids to ride the elevator up with us. I don't think we should risk the stairs."

"Agreed," Sue said. "But please hurry. I'm scared to be left alone with you-know-who."

"Should I wait here with you?" Ellen wondered.

"No. It might take both of you to convince the kids to turn in for the night and to take the elevator instead of the stairs."

"Alright then," Ellen said as she followed Tanya into the corridor.

Together, Tanya and Ellen hurried past the butler's pantry and banquet hall, past the breakfast room and salon, and to the music room, where the kids were singing *Jingle Bell Rock*.

Ellen was impressed that Lane knew that one.

"What time is it?" Ellen asked Tanya since Ellen's phone was dead.

Tanya checked her phone. "A quarter till two."

When the song ended, Ellen raised a hand in the air. "Y'all sound amazing guys, but, well, I've got some bad news."

"Is my mom okay?" Luke asked.

"She will be," Tanya said. "Her kneecap may be broken, and it's swollen up pretty bad."

"Oh, no," Alison said. "Does she need an ambulance?"

"She doesn't want one," Ellen said. "She wants to wait until morning."

Tanya nodded. "We're heading up to take her to her room, but we want you to come with us."

"What? Why?" Maya asked. "We're having so much fun."

"Yeah, Mom," Mike said. "What can *we* do about Miss Sue?"

"Well," Ellen began, "it's late, nearly two-o'clock, and…"

"So?" Alison insisted. "It's Christmas."

"Yes, but," Ellen glanced at Tanya, who shrugged, "you see, we have that champagne breakfast in the morning. We need to be down to meet the shuttle by nine o'clock sharp."

"We can rest when we're dead," Lane said playfully.

Ellen shot Tanya a worried look.

Tanya folded her arms and cleared her throat. "Well, we just ran into a security guard downstairs, and he said we can't be down here anymore."

"What?" Maya said with her brows furrowed. "My mom didn't mention anything about a curfew to me."

"Well, I wouldn't argue with that security guard," Ellen said. "We don't want to leave a bad impression on the Cecil-Vanderbilt family by breaking the rules. Now, come on, all of you. Follow us."

As Ellen led them in the opposite direction from the staircase, Lane said, "We'll take the stairs, Mom."

"No, you won't," she insisted.

"Huh?" Alison asked. "Why not, Mama?"

"There's blood on them," Tanya said quickly. "And puss. It's really gross. The security guard is sending someone over to clean it up, and I don't want us getting in the way."

"Fine," Mike said.

"Are you sure my mom is okay?" Luke asked.

"Come and see for yourself," Ellen said as they continued toward the service elevator.

Luke and Alison rushed ahead of their group. Ellen was exhausted and had to struggle to keep up with everyone.

"Mom?" Luke asked once the elevator came into view.

"I'm okay," she said, drying her eyes. "It just hurts. Come here and let me lean on you."

Luke climbed in and stood next to his mother, allowing her to lean against him and the wall of the elevator. The others climbed in, too.

"Sorry to hear about your fall," Alison said to Sue.

"Yeah, I'm glad you're okay," Lane added.

"Just get me upstairs, will you?" Sue asked.

Ellen pushed the button, and the whirring and knocking resumed as they very slowly ascended. Alcohol still lingered on the kids' breath, and it filled the elevator, making it smell like a bar.

"If it makes you feel any better, Miss Sue, I have a joke," Lane said. "What do you call Batman when he's injured?"

"I'll bite, what?" Sue asked.

"Bruised Wayne," Lane said with a grin.

"Boo," Alison said. "You stink."

"That was like a joke fart," Luke said.

"Not in the elevator, please," Sue said.

Everyone laughed.

"What was that?" Lane said suddenly. "Did someone scratch me?"

A chill snaked down Ellen's spine.

"No one scratched you, sweetie," Maya said. "I'm standing right next to you. I would have noticed."

In that moment, the elevator jerked.

"Ahhh!" they cried as it dropped a few feet before coming to a stop.

"Zelda, stop this!" Ellen cried. "Or we won't help you!"

"Mama?" Alison asked with a white face. "What's happening?"

Ellen pulled the elevator door opened only to discover they were in between floors. The second floor was just above their heads.

"Should I push the button for the second floor again and see what happens?" she asked.

"No," Tanya said. "Let's not chance it. I think there's enough room for us to crawl through that gap between the second floor and the top of the elevator door. We should get out as soon as possible."

"Speak for yourself," Sue said. "There's no way I'm getting out that way."

"What do you want us to do?" Ellen asked Sue. "You're the one who's hurt. You should decide."

More tears formed in Sue's eyes. "Well, I don't want to risk everyone's life because of me. Y'all climb out, and then I'll try pressing the button and see what happens."

"I can't fit through there either," Ellen said. "Sue and I will take our chances together."

"But Mom," Lane said. "Can't we call someone to fix the elevator?"

"I'm not standing in here any longer than I have to," Sue said. "Y'all get out before this whole thing drops again."

"Come on, Mike," Tanya said. "I'll give you a boost."

"Just be quick," Ellen said. "If the elevator drops while one of you is climbing out, well…" Ellen couldn't finish her sentence. It was too terrible to say. They could easily be maimed or killed. Ellen began to pray as hard as she could.

Tanya linked her fingers and held out her arms for Mike, who quickly put his foot in her hands before grabbing onto the second floor. Once he was out, Ellen sighed with relief.

One out. Now, please, please, please let the others make it to safety, too, she prayed.

Mike leaned over to help Seth, but Seth's foot got caught in the sleeve of Luke's tuxedo jacket. With trembling hands, Ellen got the foot free, all the while, praying harder than she had for anything in quite some time. Just as Seth cleared the elevator, the whole thing trembled.

"Ahh!" they all cried.

Ellen flinched and may have peed a little.

When she opened her eyes, she was relieved that no one was hurt. Fortunately, there was still a wide enough gap for the kids and Tanya to slide through to the second floor, but she was even more terrified than before that the elevator would drop before someone had cleared it and that that someone would be severely injured if not killed. But if they didn't climb out and they tried pushing the button, the whole thing could crash, and how could they survive such a fall?

With shaking hands, Lane linked his fingers together for Maya, who climbed out next. Ellen felt sick when it was Lane's turn. Luke linked his fingers together and helped Lane out. Then, he helped Alison. Ellen cried tears of relief when her children were safe. As Tanya linked her fingers together to help Luke, the elevator trembled again.

"Dear, Lord, please," Sue cried.

The elevator stopped shaking, and Luke went for it. Sue covered her heart with her hand and wept.

Next, Ellen linked her fingers together for Tanya. "You got this," she said to her friend. "Just move quickly, okay?"

Tanya gave her a nod before stepping into her hands and climbing out.

"What a relief," Ellen said as she wiped tears from her eyes. "That was worse than something from *The Poseidon Adventure*."

"Does everyone have rooms on the second floor?" Sue asked Tanya.

Tanya put the question to the others. Then she put her face near the opening and said, "Yes. We're all on this floor."

"Make them promise to go to bed," Ellen said.

"I will. But we're going to wait for you guys here, to make sure you get out okay."

Ellen held her finger over the button to the second floor, terrified that the elevator might drop to the sub-basement and kill them both. Aloud, she said, "Zelda Fitzgerald, just remember, if we die, so does your story."

As she pushed the button, she said a little prayer. When the elevator began to whir and knock, she took Sue's hand in hers.

"Just so you know, I love you," Ellen said.

"I know, my dear friend. I love you, too."

CHAPTER EIGHTEEN

Last Chances

Relief swept through Ellen when the elevator stopped on the second floor. Mike and Luke reached in to help Sue and Ellen out as quickly as possible. Once their feet were on solid ground, Ellen and her friends and their children expressed their gratitude over everyone making it out safely, and they exchanged hugs.

"Merry Christmas!"

"I love you!"

"Oh, thank goodness!"

"I need to sit down!" Sue cried.

"And we need to be quiet, so as not to wake the others," Ellen reminded them.

Luke and Mike helped Sue to the closest sitting area—the oak sitting room just off the hall, named for its oak wall paneling. As they crossed the room to a green damask sofa near one of two fireplaces, where a fire still crackled in the hearth, Ellen admired the square moldings in the wooden paneling and the way they contrasted with the floral designs in the cream coffered ceiling. The ceilings matched the light wooden floors laid in a herringbone pattern, while the Christmas tree was decorated in jewel tones.

Sue sighed when she finally was able to relieve the pressure on her knees. She leaned back beneath a painting of William Henry Vanderbilt and stretched her legs across the green damask sofa. Beside them, to the left of the fireplace, was an ebony cabinet on a stand that reminded Ellen of Paris. The fireplace on the opposite side of the room had a similar piece of furniture beside it.

"Are you sure we shouldn't call for an ambulance, Mom?" Luke asked Sue.

"I'm sure."

"I should go wake Nolan," Ellen said.

"Please don't," Sue insisted.

"That really needs ice," Tanya pointed out. "Isn't there any ice in this house?"

"I don't think so," Ellen said.

"What about snow?" Lane said. "Couldn't we gather some from one of the balconies?"

"Do we have anything to put it in?" Sue asked.

"I have a plastic bag for my laundry," Lane said. "I'll grab it."

"I'll go with you," Maya said.

Ellen, who had sat on the chair near Sue, stood up. "Wait. Wear this for protection." She took off her *gris gris* and put it around Lane's neck.

"Whatever, Mom," Lane said with a roll of his eyes.

Once he and Maya had gone, Ellen removed her tourmaline ring and turned to Alison. "You wear this for me, okay sweetie?"

"It's so pretty. Are you sure?"

"It's for your protection."

Alison slid on the ring and kissed Ellen on the cheek.

"Go to bed now, okay?" Ellen asked.

"Okay, Goodnight."

"Ellen, can you give Luke my *gris gris*?" Sue asked as she pulled the thin leather cord from her neck and handed it over.

Ellen took it and gave it to Luke, who put it around his neck.

"Weird, but okay," he said.

Tanya put her *gris gris* around Mike's neck and gave Seth her tourmaline ring. Then the kids said good night and Merry Christmas before heading off to their respective rooms.

Sue took out her phone. "I should write that article exonerating Zelda now."

"Why don't you dictate, and I'll write?" Ellen offered.

Sue gave her the phone, and Ellen sat back in the gold damask chair beside her. Tanya took a seat in a similar chair opposite Ellen.

"Oh, Lord," Tanya said. "What a night."

"We should have tried to help that security guard," Ellen said as tears filled her eyes. "Maybe he wasn't dead—at least, not at first. I mean, we could have saved his life. He was so young."

"We should have called the police," Tanya said. "Should we now?"

"It's too late for that," Sue pointed out. "Someone will find him soon enough. Let's write that blog article before Zelda hurts someone else."

"Oh, hell," Ellen said. "Your phone just died."

"Oh, God," Sue said.

"Tanya, mine's dead, too. Does yours have any juice?"

Tanya took out her phone. "I still have twenty percent."

"Give it to me and I'll log into my blog."

Lane and Maya returned with a plastic bag filled with snow. The bag looked like a white kitchen garbage bag. It had been filled a third of the way and tied in a knot. They placed it on Sue's swollen knee.

"Thank you. That already feels so much better."

"Goodnight," Lane said.

"And Merry Christmas," Maya added.

"Goodnight," Ellen and her friends replied.

"What do you think about Luke and Alison?" Tanya asked them.

"It can't last," Sue said. "Donald Trump and Nancy Pelosi have a better chance of having a relationship."

Ellen laughed. "I agree. What a shocker. Those two are opposites in every way."

"Well, they say opposites attract," Tanya teased.

"Okay, I'm logged in." Sue handed Tanya's phone to Ellen. Then she said, "Ready?"

"Ready," Ellen said.

"A recent visit to the Biltmore Estate in Asheville, North Carolina for the wedding of a friend resulted in a strange encounter with the ghost of Zelda Fitzgerald, whose husband is best known for his famous novel, *The Great Gatsby*."

"Slow down," Ellen complained as she typed out Sue's words. "I have fat fingers."

"Tell me when you're caught up," Sue said.

"Ellen finished typing *The Great Gatsby*. "Okay. Ready."

"The ghost was wearing a pink tutu, but don't let her innocent-looking attire fool you. She was powerful and menacing and demanded that her truth be told, or she would kill a family friend or loved one."

"Hold on," Ellen said. "Or she would kill a family friend or loved one. Okay, keep going."

"Although I am writing this article under duress, what I am saying is nonetheless true. Zelda Fitzgerald claimed that her husband Scott heavily mined her diaries and letters for material in his novels and stories."

"Wait. Heavily mined her diaries and letters . . . what came after that?"

"For material in his novels and stories," Sue repeated.

Ellen finished the sentence. "Okay."

"Stories wrote exclusively by Zelda were published under Scott's name. She also insisted that Scott made her cut material from her own novel because he wanted to use it in his, and to keep her from publishing first, he admitted her into a sanitarium, where she claimed her condition only worsened."

"Hold up," Ellen said. "Where she claimed her condition only worsened."

"That's good," Tanya said. "Why don't you stop there and hit publish? You can always add to it later."

"Good idea," Ellen said, hitting publish. She watched the site buffer for several seconds before she received an error message. "What the heck? Oh, no! It didn't publish!"

In that moment, Sue clutched her throat. Her eyes grew wide, and she stopped breathing.

Ellen and Tanya jumped to their feet.

"Zelda! Stop this!" Ellen cried. "We're trying our best to help you!"

She and Tanya passed their hands in the air around Sue's head and shoulders, but their efforts did nothing to free Sue from the spirit's grasp.

Sue's eyes began to water, and her face went from white to red.

"We have to do something!" Ellen cried.

"But what?" Tanya wanted to know.

Just then, Sammy's black lab service dog entered the sitting room from Mrs. Vanderbilt's bedroom. He ran straight across the floor to the couch where Sue was lying, and he barked ferociously at Sue. Dressed in pink pajamas, Maya's little sister Sammy ran after him.

"Marley, stop!" Sammy cried. "Stop it, boy!"

Soon her parents, Greg and Karen Stone, also wearing sleepwear and bleary-eyed expressions from having been awakened in the dead of night, entered too.

"What's going on?" Greg asked. "Sammy, get your dog under control."

Sue's face relaxed, and she took in a deep breath before she began to cough.

Sammy's dog quieted down to a whimper and sat on his haunches near Sue.

"Sue? Are you okay?" Tanya asked.

Still holding her throat, Sue nodded. "That dog saved my life."

"Is that true?" Greg asked.

"Yes," Ellen said. "Please don't be angry with him."

"What happened to your knee?" Karen asked.

"I fell on it. I think I shattered my kneecap."

"Honey, you should call Dr. Wilder," Karen told Greg.

"Please don't," Sue said. "It's what? Three o'clock on Christmas morning? Please don't bother anyone."

"Besides, Nolan, my son, is a doctor," Ellen pointed out. "We could always wake him."

"Just let me sit here until morning," Sue insisted.

"Can I help you to your room?" Greg offered.

"If it's alright with you, I'd rather not try to move again," Sue said. "At least not until morning."

"Let us know if you need anything," Karen said. "We'll be right next door."

"Thank you," Sue said. Then she turned to Sammy. "I'm so grateful to Marley."

Sammy smiled as she called her dog to her and then followed her parents to their room.

When the three friends were alone again, Ellen said, "We have no choice but to banish you-know-who."

"Agreed," Tanya said. "But how?"

"Maybe Gallatin will help us," Sue said. "He did warn us about her."

"Maybe he can show us where *The Great Gatsby* is," Tanya said.

"Or one of Fitzgerald's other works," Sue said.

Ellen pulled the dousing rods from her shoulder bag. "We can use these."

With a dousing rod in each hand, Ellen followed Tanya from the oak sitting room, through the second-floor living room, and down the corridor to the second-floor balcony of the library. At the entranceway, she and Tanya stopped and stared at the room below. It was quiet and dark. Ellen suspected the lights must be on a timer, or perhaps the ghosts had used them up.

Tanya fished the flashlight from Ellen's bag and turned it on.

Ellen took a deep breath and said, "Spirits of the other realm, we come in peace and mean no harm. We're looking for the ghost of Gallatin Roberts. Gallatin, if you're here, could you please give us a sign?"

The flashlight in Tanya's hand flickered, causing Tanya to jump.

"Geez, that scared me," Tanya said.

"Gallatin Roberts," Ellen said into the empty room. "Is that you? If so, please make the flashlight blink twice."

The flashlight flickered twice.

"It's him," Tanya whispered.

"Gallatin," Ellen continued. "We're looking for a book by F. Scott Fitzgerald. You've lived here a long time. Can you show us where we can find one of Fitzgerald's books? It could be *The Great Gatsby*, *The Sun Also Rises*, or anything else written by Fitzgerald. You can use these dousing rods like you did earlier tonight. Bring the tips closer together as I near a Fitzgerald book and point them further apart if I'm going the wrong way."

As Ellen moved toward the small spiral staircase, the rod tips moved away from one another.

She turned to Tanya, "Go back."

Ellen turned down the balcony overlooking the library below. As she walked across it, the rod tips moved together and then touched. Ellen stopped. A book from the shelf dropped at her feet.

Tanya stooped to pick it up.

"Which one is it?" Ellen asked.

"It's a book called *To Hell and Back* by Audie Murphy."

Ellen furrowed her brows. "What?"

"Do you think it's a message?" Tanya wondered.

Ellen searched the shelf from where the book had fallen to see if there were any by Fitzgerald novels nearby. She came up empty. "There's nothing here by Fitzgerald."

"I think Zelda's messing with us," Tanya whispered. "Think about it. *To Hell and Back*?"

"Great." Ellen sucked in her lips, trying to think.

"Maybe we should look for the books the old-fashioned way. You take the flashlight. I'll use my phone."

"This could take forever," Ellen complained.

"Got any better ideas?"

Ellen sighed and put away her dousing rods. Then she took the flashlight from Tanya.

"You look up here, and I'll check downstairs," Ellen said.

Ellen had barely made it to the ground level when she heard Tanya cry out. She looked up to see Tanya hanging over the railing of the balcony, the tips of her toes barely touching the ground.

"Help me, Ellen!"

Ellen rushed back up the steps, and when she reached the balcony, she had a fright. Just as Tanya was about to fall, the ghost of George Vanderbilt interceded and pulled her back to safety. He disappeared as quickly as he had appeared. Ellen ran to Tanya's side.

"Oh, my God, Tanya! That scared the heck out of me!"

Tanya was panting, trying to catch her breath. She bent over and rested her hands on her knees. "Me, too. I was sure I was going to fall. What happened?"

"You didn't see him?"

"See who?"

"George Vanderbilt saved your life!"

Tanya's mouth dropped open. Then, as tears slipped from her eyes, she said, "Thank you, George. Thank you so much."

"What's this?" Ellen noticed a book on the floor near Tanya's feet. "*The Beautiful and the Damned*, by F. Scott Fitzgerald. This is it. Let's hurry back to Sue."

<u>CHAPTER NINETEEN</u>

A Banishment Spell

Ellen and Tanya returned with the book to the oak sitting room to find Sue fast asleep. Her head leaned against the back of the green damask couch, and her mouth was wide open. Ellen was surprised her snoring hadn't disturbed the other guests.

"Don't wake her," Tanya whispered. "We can do this without her."

"Remind me what we need to do," Ellen said quietly.

"Have you got a pen?"

"I think so." Ellen fished through her bag and brought one out. She'd taken it from the room with *Authorized Personnel Only* on the door.

"We need to make a circle of protection around us," Tanya said. "The spell calls for black salt."

"Black salt?"

"You mix it with burned sage, ash, or charcoal," Tanya explained. "These fires are still going, but the one in the living room is out. Give me your shaker, and I'll go fill it."

"I'm scared for you to leave on your own. Let's go together."

They hurried to the living area, where Ellen screwed off the lid to her shaker and dipped the opened end in the bed of ash to scoop some in with the salt.

Then Ellen screwed the lid back on. "It's a good thing we're doing this. There wasn't much salt left—not enough for a circle of protection."

They hurried back to Sue's side, where they made a circle that included the front of the hearth. As always, Ellen poured it in a counterclockwise motion.

"I hope this doesn't stain the floors or the carpet," Ellen said.

"Oh, no. I didn't think of that."

"Too late. Now what?" Ellen whispered to Tanya.

"We need to write Zelda's name in the book three times. There's also a banishing rune, a banishing sigil, and a banishing pentagram we can add to strengthen the spell. Then we seal the writing with blood."

"Our blood?" Ellen asked.

"Yes."

Ellen wrote Zelda's name three times on the cover page of the book and handed it to Tanya.

"You draw."

Tanya opened the screen on her phone and copied what was called a Nyd rune. It looked like a cross, except the horizontal line was slanted down to the right. Then she drew a circle with what looked like an upside-down fishhook with claws on each side. Finally, she created a pentagram with a circle of arrows pointing counterclockwise.

A spark from the nearby fireplace popped out and onto the rug just outside of their circle of protection, where it caught fire. Ellen pulled off one of her fuzzy slippers and slapped at the flames until they died.

"That was close," Tanya said. "And I think this rug is ruined."

"Let's hurry this up," Ellen said. "What's next?"

"We need to write a command of banishment," Tanya said.

"Give it to me." Ellen took the book and pen from Tanya and wrote: *I hereby banish Zelda Fitzgerald from Biltmore House.* Then she added: *Evil spirit, leave this place. We only allow goodness and grace.*

"Now we need to seal it with blood," Tanya said. "Do you have a safety pin or something we can use to prick our fingers?"

Ellen shook her head. "No, but I saw a paperclip on the floor in the living room. I'll be right back."

"I'm coming with you."

They stepped out of the circle of protection and hurried back to the living room, where Ellen found the paperclip. When she bent over to pick it up, she felt hands at her neck, choking her. She clutched her throat and, with wide eyes, turned to Tanya for help. She couldn't speak, couldn't breathe. Tanya flailed around her, trying to ward off the evil spirit, but nothing worked. Ellen fell to her knees, on the verge of passing out. Tanya took Ellen by the hand and practically dragged her back to the sitting room and into their circle of protection, where Ellen was finally released from the chokehold.

Ellen gulped air. "Oh, my God."

Sue opened her eyes. "What happened?"

Ellen and Tanya caught her up to speed.

"I dropped the paperclip," Ellen said. "So now what do we do?"

"I draw blood every time I bite off a cuticle," Sue said. "Can't we just do that?"

"You want us to use our teeth to draw our own blood?" Tanya asked with incredulity.

"Yes," Sue said. "Don't be a baby."

Ellen pressed her right thumb to her teeth and gnawed. It wasn't as easy as Sue made it out to be. She had to tear at a few layers of skin before she found blood.

"This is so gross," Tanya said.

"It's for an important cause," Ellen said. "Just remember that."

They each pressed a dab of their blood onto the page where Ellen and Tanya had written and drawn the necessary marks.

The three friends were startled when something big flew toward them from the opposite end of the room. They screamed and covered their faces. The object dropped on the floor just outside of their circle of protection, on the burnt part of the rug. It was a bronze figure of an American revolutionary soldier.

"The moon must have given Zelda a lot of power," Tanya murmured.

Greg Stone opened the door from Mrs. Vanderbilt's bedroom. "What happened?"

Another bronze figure was hurled toward him. He ducked and it hit the wall behind him.

"Go back to your room," Ellen cried. "We've got this!"

She spoke with much more confidence than she felt.

Greg did as he was told, and a framed photo slammed against the door just as he closed it behind him.

"Hurry, Tanya," Sue said. "What's next?"

Tanya took her finger and smeared the blood in a counterclockwise motion while she said, "I bind the ghost of Zelda Fitzgerald to this book."

Then she tossed the book into the fire as she said, "I hereby banish Zelda Fitzgerald from Biltmore House. Evil spirit, leave this place. We only allow goodness and grace."

They watched in silence as the book burned. Ellen could sense the pressure in the room changing. It felt less oppressive, less negative, and brighter by the second.

"We need to cover the ashes of the book with the black salt," Tanya said.

"I'll do it." Ellen carried the saltshaker to the hearth and sprinkled the black salt over the ashes. As she did, she said, "I hereby banish Zelda Fitzgerald from Biltmore House. Evil spirit, leave this place. We only allow goodness and grace."

Then she turned to her friends. "It's done."

"Do you think it worked?" Tanya asked Ellen.

Ellen took a deep breath and stepped outside the circle of protection. When nothing accosted her, she said, "I'm going to bed. I'm totally exhausted."

"Me, too," Tanya said. Then, turning to Sue, added, "Are you sure you don't want help to your room?"

"Just leave me," she said. "I can sleep here as well as anyplace. But would you mind filling the bag with fresh snow before you go to bed?"

"I'll help," Ellen said.

Tanya picked up the white kitchen garbage bag of melted snow. "Where should we go? I don't think there are any balconies on this level."

"There's one off my bedroom, but I don't want to risk waking Brian."

"Should we go down to the loggia?"

"I suppose so." To Sue, she said, "We'll be right back."

Ellen followed Tanya from the oak sitting room through the second living area.

"I assume we're taking the stairs," Tanya said as she headed toward the grand spiral staircase.

"Absolutely. No more elevators for me for a while."

They descended to the first floor. The main hall was dark, as was the tapestry room. The cold air chilled them as they stepped out onto the loggia beneath the bright moonlight.

There was plenty of snow on the terrace to gather into the bag for Sue.

"I wish I had gloves," Tanya said as she untied the bag and emptied it of the melted snow.

"It's freezing out here," Ellen agreed. "You hold the bag down, and I'll shovel in the snow."

When it was a third full, Tanya asked, "You think that's good?"

"Yeah. I think so. Let's go."

As they stood to go, Ellen heard a piercing sound from below. She and Tanya stood still and listened. At first, she thought it was the howling of the wind. Then she thought it might be a coyote. But when it rang out for a third time, she recognized the low, raspy cackle from the throat of Zelda Fitzgerald.

Ellen looked over the railing to see the ballerina as a full-bodied apparition standing on the snowy hillside below.

"You may have banished me from the house," the phantom shouted, "but I'll be here waiting on the grounds when you come out."

Tanya stepped back and covered her mouth. "I could cry right now."

Feeling frustrated, Ellen took a deep breath and stepped closer to the railing, to be sure she was in full view of the specter below. Ellen hated the ghost for what she had done—for killing the security guard and hurting and tormenting her and her friends. But Ellen knew that her job of helping spirits to find closure was a calling that extended far beyond what she—what Ellen—wanted. She wouldn't be the judge and jury for the ghosts she encountered but an instrument for the divine. It gave Ellen great satisfaction and a sense of purpose to know that the universe could use her for the betterment of all souls. Plus, although Zelda had been an absolute heel, she, like every soul, deserved to rest in peace after spending so many years in a kind of hell on earth.

"Go ahead and make your threats, Zelda Fitzgerald," Ellen finally said. "I know that there is good in you and that you deserve to have your story told. I promise that I will be your advocate. I will help Sue to publish her article on her blog, and I will look for other ways to spread the word about how you were wronged by your husband. I will make sure the world knows what a creative, passionate, and gifted person you were. I give you my word."

From such a height, Ellen couldn't be certain, but she thought Zelda was shedding tears. The ballerina curtsied and disappeared.

"That was some speech," Tanya said, as she followed Ellen into the house carrying the bag of snow.

"I think I finally understand Shiri's tarot reading. She was right. Spot on."

Together, they took the stairs up to the oak sitting room, where Sue had fallen asleep again. They gently balanced the bag of snow on her knee, which startled her awake, but they whispered goodnight, and she closed her eyes, returning to sleep.

Before heading off to her room, Ellen reached out and gave Tanya a hug. "Merry Christmas, my dear friend. I love you."

"I love you, too, Ellen. Merry Christmas."

"No making out in the sitting room," Sue said with one eye open.

Tanya and Ellen laughed.

"She's onto us," Tanya said.

Ellen leaned over and kissed the top of Sue's head. "I can make out wherever I want."

CHAPTER TWENTY

Champagne Breakfast

By the time Ellen slipped beneath the red velvet duvet beside Brian and plugged in her phone to recharge on the nightstand, it was nearly four in the morning. She'd need to be up in four hours to get ready for their special champagne breakfast and winery tour.

As exhausted as she was, she had a hard time falling asleep. Brian hadn't seemed to move since she left his side nearly five hours ago. She took deep, slow breaths, and tried to relax, but the image of the young security guard slumped against the boiler room wall with his legs sprawled out on the floor wouldn't leave her mind. What a terrible waste of life. She should have done something instead of being too afraid of getting caught. She might have saved him. She prayed to God to forgive her for her part in his death. She would be forever scarred by this night. Instead of remembering it as the night that her son was happily married, it will be the night that she was culpable for a young man's death. Tears gathered in her eyes, and she wept into her pillow, trying not to wake Brian. It seemed a long time to Ellen before she finally drifted off to sleep.

Ellen blinked against the early morning light shining in through the sheer curtains over the balcony windows. Brian had curled himself around her back and was kissing her shoulder.

"Good morning," he said. "And Merry Christmas."

"Merry Christmas. What time is it?"

"Nearly eight."

"I feel like my head just hit the pillow. Is it really that late?"

He kissed her shoulder again. "What a sleepyhead. You've had nine hours, and you're still tired?"

She rolled over to face him. "Try less than four."

He lifted his dark, bushy brows, his gray eyes worried. "Why? What happened?"

"Oh, Brian." She shook her head. "I have so much to tell you. We had such an adventure last night."

"All good, I hope."

"Not all," she said thinking of the young security guard.

He kissed her cheek and hopped out of bed. "I'm looking forward to hearing all about it during our trip home. It'll make the flight go by faster. I'm going to take a quick bath."

Ellen closed her eyes hoping to get a few more winks in before she had to get up and get dressed, but now that she was awake, sleep would not return.

"Sue!" she said aloud. To Brian, she hollered, "I need to check on Sue. I'll be right back."

When she reached the oak sitting room in her robe and slippers, she found Nolan already there examining his patient. Poor Sue had dark rings beneath her eyes, but at least her knee looked improved. The swelling had gone down from the size of a cantaloupe to that of an orange.

"Merry Christmas, Mom," Nolan said as Ellen entered.

"Merry Christmas," she replied. "How's our patient?"

"Tired but the pain's better," Sue said.

"The good news is that I don't think her kneecap is broken, though I'd still get it x-rayed, just to confirm," Nolan said. "The bad news is that it's badly bruised and she really should stay off it for a few days. I don't think she should fly back today."

Sue chuckled. "You think Maya's Vanderbilt relatives can make me a more permanent guest here?"

Ellen scoffed. "Oh, sure. I'll have all your things brought over, and you can move right in."

"Sounds good to me," Sue said. "Let Tom and the kids know that they're welcome to visit."

"Where is Tom, by the way?" Ellen asked.

"He went with Greg to see about finding me a wheelchair. They don't know that I'm staying put—though, actually, after the elevator trouble we had last night, I don't think I want to live here after all."

"I wish you could stay put," Nolan said. "It would be the best thing for you. But a wheelchair will certainly help."

"Did someone call for a wheelchair?" Greg said, as he led Tom into the sitting room.

Tom was pushing an old-fashioned wheelchair across the room. Made of rattan, wood, and steel, it had four wheels—two large wheels in the back and two small ones in the front—and it had a handle in the back reminding Ellen of a baby buggy.

"Where did you find that old thing?" Nolan asked.

"More to the point," Sue began. "Will it hold?"

"I'm sure it will," Tom said. "It's quite sturdy."

"It's an antique," Ellen said, worried that using it might ruin its value.

"It suits our needs," Greg said. "Our night watchman found it in one of the storage rooms downstairs in the sub-basement."

"Night watchman?" Ellen asked.

"Yes," Greg said with a nod. "He was watching over the place for us last night. It was a condition for our overnight stay. By the way, that was crazy last night. Did I imagine that figurine coming at me? Or was I sleepwalking?"

"You didn't imagine it," Ellen said. "We were dealing with an angry ghost."

"But no worries," Sue said. "We banished her."

Ellen didn't add that the ghost of Zelda Fitzgerald was still haunting the grounds outside the house.

"I've never seen anything like that," Greg said. "How fascinating your lives must be."

Tom's face reddened. "You didn't mention any of that to me, Sue."

"I planned to," she said. "I just haven't had the opportunity."

"Oh, speak of the devil," Greg said. "We were just talking about you, Jacob."

The young security guard from the previous night who Ellen had been sure was dead entered the room. "Is that all you need, Mr. Stone?"

"Yes, Jacob. Thanks so much. You're free to go."

"Merry Christmas, everyone," Jacob said.

"Merry Christmas," the men replied.

Ellen, who had been gaping at the young man since he'd entered, snapped out of it and said, "Merry Christmas."

She was still processing that this young man whom she had mourned all night was standing right in front of her.

"Mom?" Nolan asked.

She gave him a smile and a shake of her head.

Then, turning to Sue, Nolan asked, "Has your pain worsened?"

Sue wiped tears from her cheeks. "I'm just tired. I'll be alright."

As Jacob was leaving the oak sitting room, Tanya entered with her husband Dave. At the sight of Jacob alive and well, she jumped back, covered her mouth, and shrieked.

"I'm sorry, ma'am," Jacob said. "I didn't mean to startle you."

Tanya shot looks of incredulity toward Ellen and Sue before gathering her wits about her. "No apology needed. I'm just an anxious person who's easily startled."

"Well, Merry Christmas," Jacob said as he continued from the room.

"Merry Christmas," Dave said.

Once the security guard had gone, Ellen began to laugh. She was hysterically happy. So happy and relieved. Sue and Tanya caught the giggle bug and joined her.

"What's so funny?" Nolan asked.

But the three women couldn't stop laughing long enough to explain.

After a bath and a change of clothes, Ellen felt rejuvenated and excited about touring the winery before their champagne breakfast. As instructed, she and Brian left their luggage in the room and headed to the spiral staircase. Lane and Maya were already descending the stairs ahead, as were members of the Biltmore staff, who had come to prepare the house for public touring.

Tanya caught up with Ellen as they neared the main floor and said, "I asked one of the workers about Linda Bracken."

"Good thinking," Ellen said. "Did you find out anything?"

"The house opens at noon today. She'll be here then."

As they reached the main level, Ellen asked, "How will we find her? Did you get a phone number or anything?"

"The person I spoke to said there was no way to contact Linda directly. She recommended that we go online and request a private tour with her."

"We have to buy a tour to talk to her?"

Brian lifted his bushy brows. "You're going on another tour today?"

Ellen sucked in her lips.

"We may as well, Ellen," Tanya said. "I have a feeling we're going to need a lot of her time."

"True."

Brian scratched his chin. "Do I want to know what you're talking about?"

"I promise to tell you the whole story later, but I'm thinking about staying behind with Sue for another day or two. Would you be terribly disappointed if I did?"

"What about our Christmas tonight?" he asked.

"I really don't want to miss it," Ellen admitted, "but I don't feel I have a choice."

"That's disappointing, but I understand," Brian said as he kissed the side of her cheek.

"Does that mean you're staying, too?" Dave asked Tanya.

"I think so," Tanya said. "Is that okay?"

Dave laughed. "Hell, yeah. Extended vacation time for me."

"Oh, stop," Tanya said with a grin. "Don't pretend you won't be sad that I can't be there tonight with you and the kids."

As they exited the house, Tanya said to Ellen, "Maybe we could ask for the basement tour, and when we have her alone with the trunk, we can tell her what happened."

"I hope she believes us. She may decide to call the cops."

"The cops?" Brian asked. "Okay, now you're scaring me."

"The ghost of Linda's grandfather led us to his trunk in the basement, to his autobiography," Ellen explained. "We had to pick the lock."

"The ghost picked the lock," Tanya clarified.

"But whether Linda believes that or not, we won't know till we tell her," Ellen said just as Sue and Tom caught up to them.

"I don't know what else to do," Tanya said. "The private tour was my best idea."

"It's a good idea, Tanya," Ellen said. "Let's do it."

"Do what?" Sue wanted to know.

Tanya and Ellen caught Sue up on their newest plan.

"I agree. It's a good plan," Sue said. "And hopefully now that I posted the Zelda article, we won't get any more harassment from her."

"We need to help her cross over," Tanya said. "Do y'all think that's possible?"

"Baby steps," Ellen said. "Let's get through our talk with Linda and go from there."

Although snow still covered the landscape, the blue sky was clear, and the sun warmed everything beneath it, chasing away the chill. Ellen found her brother, Jody, and his family already waiting for the trolley that would take them to Antler Hill Village, five miles away. She was wishing them all a Merry Christmas and asking how they slept when Nolan and Taylor emerged from the house with Bri.

"There she is," Ellen cried with a wave to her granddaughter. "Merry Christmas! Come give Nana a hug!"

On the heels of Nolan and Taylor were Alison and Luke.

"Merry Christmas, Mom," Alison said.

"It's back to Mom again, hmm, sweet girl?" Ellen asked as she embraced her daughter.

"What do you mean?" Alison asked.

"While you were drunk, you called me Mama."

"I did?"

"Yes, you did. And I liked it," Ellen said with a laugh. "It reminded me of when you were little."

"Okay, Mama." Alison kissed Ellen's cheek. "Merry Christmas."

Ellen gave her daughter another hug. "Merry Christmas, my sweet girl."

As the other guests from the wedding made their way to the front of Biltmore House, they shared their Christmas greetings and talked about how much they enjoyed the wedding, reception, and stay at the grandest house they'd ever seen. During these joyful exchanges, Ellen noticed that Ted and Gayle Stone were talking with James and Melissa Dresden. Ellen sucked in air and covered her mouth, hoping there wouldn't be another scene. She prayed they wouldn't ruin Christmas morning with their bickering.

Her prayers were interrupted by the arrival of the Biltmore trolley. While Tom helped Sue at the back with the handicap entrance, Ellen followed the other guests in through one of three side doors. Inside, they found cute wooden benches and an old-timey feel. As she boarded,

Ellen glanced around for the two sets of grandparents. She was shocked when Ted and Gayle took seats directly in front of James and Melissa. What was going on?

A few minutes later, they arrived at Antler Hill Village where a fountain, shops, restaurants, the village hotel, and the winery were located. The trolley came to a stop before the winery, and the guests were invited to step off.

Patricia, the wedding coordinator, met them at a set of wooden doors beneath a sign that read *Biltmore Winery Est. 1985*. After giving them some history of the winery—it had once been the famous Biltmore dairy—she led them into an underground tunnel that was filled with strings of floor-to-ceiling white lights.

"How magical," Tanya, who was just behind Ellen and Brian, said. "It's like we've entered a portal to the fairy dimension."

So as not to slow down the rest of their group, Ellen and her friends and their spouses took up the rear. They followed the guests through the winding tunnel and into the fermentation room, where tanks and barrels were filled with fermenting wine. According to Patricia, some wine required French oak barrels and other steel tanks.

From there, the group was led into the labeling room, where the bottles were labeled via a machine and conveyor belt. Then, they were shown how the bottles were corked and stored.

Patricia told the wedding guests more about the dairy farm's history, ending with, "You have just been through what was once the poop shoot."

Laughter filled the tunnel as they followed Patricia uphill into an expansive wine-tasting room with an installation of golden orbs appearing to float overhead like champagne bubbles. They were each allowed to choose seven different wines to sample before breakfast.

"Which do you like best?" Ellen asked Lane, who had been standing at the bar with Maya beside her and Brian during the sampling.

"The Sangiovese, for sure," Lane said. "What about you, Mom?"

"I'm a Chardonnay girl," she said, "though the Christmas wine was also good."

"Too sweet for me," Brian said. "I prefer Merlot." Then he asked Lane and Maya, "So what do you think of married life so far?"

"So far so good," Maya said. "Ask us again in a few months."

Lane threw his head back and guffawed. "Come on, dude. No negative vibes allowed."

"You call your girl a dude?" Brian asked with a laugh.

"It's my nickname, apparently," Maya said.

"Hey, I thought y'all wanted equality," Lane said.

"Well, you know what they say about the two cell phones who married," Brian began. "The reception was terrific."

Ellen rolled her eyes and laughed. "Not bad."

"The florists who married weren't as lucky," Brian said. "It was an arranged marriage."

"You're on a roll!" Maya said gleefully.

"I looked up some marriage puns before your wedding but never had a chance to use them on anyone," he explained.

"Do you have any more?" Lane asked.

"Well, they say it's been ten years since the invisible man married the invisible woman, and their kids are nothing to look at either."

Suddenly, Maya's face changed. Her jaw went slack, and her eyes grew wide.

"Dude, it wasn't that bad," Lane said.

"It's not that," she said. "Look."

Ellen followed Maya's gaze to see Ted Stone and James Dresden shaking hands. Then James opened his arms and went in for a hug.

"Oh my God," Ellen said.

Maya lifted her brows. "It's a Christmas miracle."

From the wine-tasting room, the wedding guests were led through another winding underground tunnel, this one marked with soft candlelight in lanterns on beds of white rose petals, to the champagne cellar. To Ellen, it looked like a dining hall from a magical castle. The soft, shimmering lights on the stone walls from chandeliers, sconces, and candlelight gave the room a romantic feel, as did the sheer, champagne-colored fabric that created a focal point on the back wall.

As everyone looked for their places, Melissa Dresden came up to Ellen with eyes full of tears.

"I want to thank you and your friends for your help last night," she said. "I was up all night talking to James, and then we spoke all morning with Ted and Gayle."

"I thought I saw you talking," Ellen said. "That's wonderful news."

"I never would have thought in a million years that we could be at peace with each other," she said as tears fell down her cheeks. "I just can't believe it. James and Ted were best friends growing up. They've missed out on so many years together, but now's there's a chance they can reconnect and be friends again."

"Now your sister can find peace, too," Ellen said.

"Do you think so?"

"My friends and I are staying for a couple of extra days—mainly because Sue needs to stay off her knee before the flight home. But we plan to wrap up some unfinished business, and that includes helping your sister to cross over to the other side."

"Really?" Melissa gave Ellen a hug. "Thank you. And bless you and your friends for the work you do."

As Ellen found her seat beside Brian and across from Sue and Tanya, she felt lighter and merrier and extremely happy. She glanced across the room at her loved ones and was pleased to see their smiles, laughter, and holiday cheer.

After the champagne was poured and the fluffy French toast, eggs, and sausage served, James Dresden stood up and said, "On behalf of the Cecil-Vanderbilt family, I'd like to wish all of you a Merry Christmas and

Happy New Year. Please raise your glasses and join me in one more toast to the bride and groom and to new beginnings."

Everyone lifted their glasses and said in unison, "To the bride and groom and to new beginnings."

CHAPTER TWENTY-ONE

Linda Bracken

After a heartfelt goodbye to their family and friends at the winery, Ellen, Sue, and Tanya checked into separate rooms at Biltmore Inn, a few minutes' drive from Antler Hill Village. Like Biltmore House, the Inn dominated the landscape, including the mountains surrounding it. Also made of limestone with a contrasting gray tiled roof, what the Inn lacked in towers, spires, and gables, it made up for in mountain views, premium amenities, and beautiful interior details reminiscent of Vanderbilt's house.

Although the décor of the rooms wasn't nearly as lavish as the Louis XV room, it was nonetheless beautiful with its dark wooden furniture, cream linens, and ivory damask wallpaper and drapes. Ellen and her friends took three connected rooms, each with their own baths. They needed to be connected so that Tanya and Ellen could help Sue getting in and out of her chair when she needed to use the facilities.

It had been heartbreaking for Ellen to stay behind on Christmas day, knowing that the rest of her family would be gathering at her home in San Antonio that evening to dine and open presents without her. She'd been looking forward to seeing the expressions on the faces of her children and granddaughter when they opened their gifts, and she'd looked forward to more intimate time with them. Lane and Maya had even postponed leaving for their honeymoon to be there with her, and now they were celebrating without her.

But Sue needed a few days before flying home, and Ellen and Tanya had agreed that they should stay, despite Tom's offer to do so instead. They encouraged Tom to go and be with the rest of his family while they took care of Sue because they felt they could use their extra time in Asheville wisely, even though they desperately missed their families.

It hadn't been easy to talk Tom out of it. All the husbands had offered to remain behind for one more day, but it seemed wrong to cancel their family Christmases.

"You'd be saving Christmas if you went," Ellen had argued.

Just before noon, Ellen, Sue, and Tanya met in the hotel lobby to take the shuttle from Biltmore Inn to the main house to meet with Linda Bracken for their private tour. It took a while for the wheelchair lift in back to get Sue up and into the vehicle, but otherwise, the shuttle ride was smooth sailing.

The front lawn peeked through the blanket of snow that was gradually melting beneath the afternoon sun, shining brightly in a clear sky. Although the temperature had returned to a comfortable fifty-five degrees, Ellen was surprised by how many people were on the estate on Christmas day. As they walked the long stretch from the shuttle drop-off point toward the front of the house, they passed dozens of other tourists.

"I wonder if we could rent an electric chair," Tanya, who was pushing Sue, said.

Sue chuckled. "Why? Who do you want to fry?"

"You know what I mean. An electric *wheel*chair."

"This isn't a theme park," Sue said.

"I doubt she meant we'd rent one from the Biltmore people, Sue," Ellen said. "Maybe there's a company that does it."

"If there isn't, that could be a solid business idea," Tanya said. "I'm sure Sue isn't the only one who's been visiting out of town and needed one temporarily."

Ellen gave Tanya a sideways glance. "Are you wanting to start a new business?"

Tanya shrugged. "No. But someone should do it."

"I don't think this happens to enough people to warrant such a business, but I could be wrong," Sue said. "And if there isn't one, maybe we could steal a scooter from a local grocery store. Don't most grocers have them for their handicapped shoppers these days?"

"Stealing is just the thing I'd like to do on Christmas day," Ellen teased.

"You've done it before," Sue pointed out. "Remember that can of cranberries when we were renovating the Gold house?"

Ellen frowned and rolled her eyes. "How could I forget?"

Tanya laughed. "Oh, Ellen. She's just teasing you."

"Speaking of Christmas," Sue said. "I'm sorry to have ruined yours."

"You haven't ruined anything," Tanya said.

"That's right," Ellen said. "It's not your fault. Besides, I'm going to Facetime with them, so it won't be that bad."

"This is better anyway," Tanya said. "Otherwise, we would have had to fly back here."

"But it's Christmas," Sue said with a frown. "I was looking forward to spending it at home tonight. Weren't you?"

"Of course, we're disappointed," Ellen admitted. "But it isn't your fault, and we may as well make the best of it."

"As a consolation, I'd really like to resolve the case of Gallatin Roberts," Tanya said. "I want to make sure he finds peace. It would be nice to have another Christmas miracle, wouldn't it?"

"It was a miracle for the grandparents, but we still need to help Melinda Brown," Ellen pointed out. "And Zelda Fitzgerald, if possible."

"We need to prepare ourselves," Sue said. "Zelda might not want peace. She's become so vindictive, you know?"

Tanya nodded. "Yeah. She might be past saving. But we have to try."

"Agreed," Ellen said. "Not just for her sake, but for the sakes of her future victims."

Sue nodded. "That's true. And there will be future victims if we don't intervene."

A line had formed near the entrance, where the lion statues stood guard. Tanya pushed Sue in the old-fashioned wheelchair toward the end of the line, and Ellen followed.

Once inside, they were met by their docent, Linda Bracken, at the check-in line.

"Hello there," Linda said as she led them through the main hall toward the grand staircase. "You look familiar. Weren't you in yesterday's wedding tour?"

"Yes," Ellen said. "I guess we didn't get enough."

"One day is never enough," Linda agreed. "Is there a part of the house that you're most interested in learning about today?"

"The basement," Sue said. "Can we start there?"

"Of course. Right this way, to the elevator."

The mention of the elevator made Ellen's heart speed up, and a sweat broke out on her forehead. They followed Linda into the main elevator, which was a relief to Ellen, because she doubted that she could ever step foot into the service elevator again. As Linda pulled the door closed and pushed the button for the basement, Ellen reminded herself that Zelda had been banished from the house, and it was she who had caused the elevator trouble last night. Despite this reminder, she prayed fervently as they yielded to the knocks and whirring of one-hundred-year-old machinery.

Once Linda had pulled open the door and they were safely in the corridor, Ellen released the breath she'd been holding.

"Shall we start here with the men's dressing rooms?" Linda asked. "Or we could start on the other end with the laundry and folding rooms."

"Let's do that," Sue said. "The laundry and folding, if you don't mind."

"Of course not," Linda said. "This way."

When they reached the closet door at the end of the corridor, where Gallatin's trunk was stored, Ellen asked, "Can you show us what's in this room?"

"Oh, that's just a storage closet," Linda said. "There's nothing of interest in there."

"Actually, there is," Sue said.

Linda stopped and turned to face Sue. "I beg your pardon?"

"There's something we need to talk to you about, Linda," Ellen said. "You see, we're paranormal investigators, and last night during the wedding, the ghost of your grandfather, Gallatin Roberts, appeared to me asking for help."

Linda gaped and said nothing for five full seconds.

"I know it's a lot to take in," Tanya said.

"What are you trying to pull?" Linda asked with her eyes narrowed. "I don't believe in that nonsense. So, what is it you really want?"

A couple carrying their handheld audio tour devices walked past, so Ellen waited for them to turn the corner before saying, "He wants to be exonerated, Linda. He didn't give Central Bank the millions just before they went bankrupt. Someone else did."

Linda backed up. "What makes you think that?"

"He wrote about it in his autobiography," Sue explained. "The diaries are in his trunk, which is being stored in that room."

Linda's face paled. "How did you know that? Is this some kind of joke? Have I been set up on a reality television show?"

Ellen lifted her palms in the air, like a criminal at gunpoint. "This isn't a joke, and you haven't been set up." She reached into her pocket. "He appeared to me in the banquet hall last night and gave me this note." She handed him the note in which the ghost had requested a meeting at the swimming pool.

"This is ridiculous," Linda said. "I'm not listening to any of this. I'll need to escort you from the building now, or I'll have to call security."

"Please give us a few minutes to prove to you that we aren't lying," Sue said.

"I don't see how you can," Linda said with a sigh.

"We met him at the pool as he asked," Ellen said. "And that's when he told us about the trunk with his diaries. We used this set of dousing rods so he could lead us to the trunk. He led us to this room, and once inside, he used the end of this rod to pick the lock and open the trunk."

"You broke into his trunk?" Linda asked with her mouth gaping.

"We didn't have to," Sue said. "He did it for us. And we read his diaries."

"We found the proof he asked for," Tanya said. "Don't you want to exonerate your grandfather?"

Linda opened the closet door and made her way to the corner to the trunk. The padlock lay on the floor beside it, where Ellen and her friends had left it.

"My grandmother told us never to open it," Linda said. "It hasn't been opened since before my grandfather's death."

"Then why is it here?" Ellen wanted to know.

"I didn't know what else to do with it, so I donated it. Another historian and I were going to eventually go through it. I just kept putting it off."

"Don't put it off a moment longer," Sue said. "Your grandfather can't find peace until you clear his name."

Tears welled in Linda's eyes, and her hands began to shake.

"There, there," Sue said. "I didn't mean to make you cry."

"It's too much," Linda said as the floodgates opened.

"Do you mind if I open the trunk and show you the diaries?" Ellen asked.

Linda nodded. "Fine."

Ellen opened the lid and took up the diaries, which she and her friends had returned the night before. She found the one that Tanya had skimmed. Ellen leafed through the pages.

When she found the passage that she was looking for, she handed it over to Linda. "Read this."

Linda took the diary and read the page Ellen had pointed out. When she'd finished, Linda covered her mouth as more tears spilled from her eyes.

"Don't you agree that's proof?" Sue asked. "Look at the date for the entry. He wasn't indicted until 1931, and this entry is from October of 1930."

"I'm not sure if it will stand up to scrutiny," Linda said. "Someone could accuse me of writing it. How do you know I didn't?"

"You said the trunk hasn't been opened since your grandfather's death," Tanya pointed it.

"That's true, but who will believe me?" she asked.

"We can testify in a court of law, under oath," Sue said. "If necessary, you can take a lie detector test. We all can. And there are handwriting experts who can analyze the books and authenticate them by comparing them to the other documents in the trunk."

"Couldn't my grandfather had planted it, in hopes of covering himself?"

"If that were the case, he wouldn't have killed himself, would he have?" Tanya offered. "He would have shown the diary to the court."

"I wonder why he didn't," Sue said.

"Maybe he forgot he'd written it," Ellen said. "Or perhaps he didn't want to incriminate someone who hadn't been brought up in charges. Who knows? Maybe an investigation into this other person will yield something."

"Do you really think it's possible to exonerate him?" Linda asked.

"Absolutely," Ellen said. "And the process begins with you."

CHAPTER TWENTY-TWO

A Christmas Surprise

From Biltmore House, Ellen and Tanya ordered a handicap accessible van to transport Sue to the emergency room for x-rays. They had considered waiting until after Christmas, when Sue might be seen by Karen and Greg's doctor, but there was no guarantee he'd be able to squeeze her in with such short notice, and they didn't want to delay their return to San Antonio any longer than was necessary.

The ER was busier than one might expect on a Christmas day. They waited for two hours for Sue to be seen, and another forty-five minutes for the x-rays to be taken. Since they'd barely had four hours of sleep the night before, they found it difficult to stay awake through the ordeal. Rather than make them wait further for the radiologist, the nurse took Sue's number and said she would call with the report. Meanwhile, Sue was given a prescription for painkillers and was told to stay off the knee as much as possible and to ice it every four hours.

By the time they returned to Biltmore Inn, it was after four o'clock.

As they took the elevator up to their rooms, Ellen said, "Why don't we order room service tonight? There's no reason why we shouldn't celebrate Christmas together, don't you think?"

"I agree," Sue said. "Let's wait until after we've all had a chance to Facetime our families. Would a late meal be alright with y'all?"

"Sounds good to me," Tanya said.

"Me, too," Ellen agreed. "I think I'll take a shower and have a nap before calling Brian. Do you need help in the bathroom Sue?"

"I'll let you know," she said. "The painkiller has made all the difference. I think I can manage."

"Try not to put any weight on the knee," Tanya said. "Just because you can't feel the pain doesn't mean it's healed."

"Yes, Doctor," Sue said. "Oh, but I will need ice. Would one of you mind?"

"I'll do it," Tanya offered.

"I'll get it the next time," Ellen promised.

When Ellen reached her room, she found a card on her bed addressed to her. She opened it to find an invitation that read: *Please join me in the Vanderbilt Ballroom at 7 p.m. for Christmas dinner. Casual attire.*

Bewildered by the invitation, she knocked on Sue's door.

"Come in," Sue said.

"I got an invitation to dinner tonight," she said. "Do you know anything about it?"

"I did, too," Sue said. "And no, I have no idea who sent it."

Just then, Tanya came in from the other side of Sue's room. "Hello? Oh, hey, guys. I just found an invitation to dinner tonight. Did you get one?"

"We did," Ellen said. "But who sent it?"

"I don't know, but do we have to go?" Tanya wondered. "I was looking forward to staying in and Facetiming the family tonight. I really miss them."

"Me, too," Sue said. "We didn't spend as much time together as I'd hoped this weekend."

"I suppose we don't have to go," Ellen said. "Should we just ignore it?"

"It's really strange," Tanya said. "Do you think maybe Maya's parents arranged for this when they heard we were staying behind?"

"Oh, that could be," Ellen said. "Maybe they felt sorry for us and wanted to throw us a special dinner."

"In that case, it sounds like we have no choice but to go," Sue said. "But I think I need a nap first."

"Me, too," Ellen said. "I'm exhausted."

"We could always go and then excuse ourselves early to Facetime our families," Tanya said. "I'm sure Maya's parents, or whoever arranged for this, will understand."

"Let's plan to go down a few minutes before seven," Sue said. "We can meet here, in my room."

"See you then," Ellen said.

Ellen showered and dried her hair before sliding beneath the crisp, clean sheets of her hotel bed. She thought she'd have no trouble falling asleep, but she couldn't stop thinking about her children and granddaughter at home with Brian sharing their Christmas cheer without her. After enduring the terrifying incident in the elevator, she wanted more than ever to be with them. But she felt responsible for Sue's injury and hadn't wanted Tom to have to cancel his flight. And she hadn't wanted to leave without trying once more to help the ghosts at Biltmore find peace.

She tossed and turned for over an hour before she finally gave up, got dressed, fixed her hair and makeup, and then watched television until it was time to meet her friends in Sue's room.

"Ready?" she asked Sue and Tanya when she popped into Sue's room at 6:55 p.m.

"Ready to meet our mystery hosts," Sue said with a laugh. "But Tom is calling me to Facetime in half an hour, so I may not stay long."

"Let's just eat and run," Tanya said as she followed Ellen, who was pushing Sue, out into the hall.

They took the elevator down to the Vanderbilt Ballroom. Ellen clenched her teeth during the ride down, feeling a little PTSD. When they exited into the lobby, she released the breath she'd been holding.

Tanya followed the signs to the ballroom, this time letting Ellen push Sue. When Tanya opened the ballroom doors, they had a shock. There was a long buffet table filled with food, and three dining tables already set. The ballroom had been transformed into three cozy sitting areas around three fireplaces. Each had a Christmas tree, two sofas, a loveseat, and two chairs, with a coffee table and a mound of presents. Best of all, their respective families were already comfortably sitting and waiting to surprise them. They jumped up and welcomed Ellen and her friends with hugs and kisses as Christmas carols played softly over the speakers.

Ellen could find no words as each of her family members kissed her.

"What in the world?" Tanya cried gleefully.

"How did you manage this?" Sue wanted to know.

Brian laughed at how shocked Ellen was.

"I hope this is okay with you," he said.

"I couldn't be happier," she said as tears spilled down her cheeks. "I don't know how you did it."

"We had the kids stay behind and prepare the room," Dave explained. "We husbands flew home to collect all of the gifts."

"I thought I saw Maya earlier," Sue said. "I just thought she and Lane had decided to stay an extra night."

"I thought you saw me," Maya said. "I was so worried I gave it all away."

"How did you get all the presents here in time?" Ellen asked.

"Brian's jet," Tom added. "It was the only way we could make it in time."

"I still can't believe this!" Tanya said, her blue eyes gleaming.

"I felt like we were flying Santa's sleigh with all the presents we had crammed in my small jet," Brian said. To Bri, he added, "Now I know how Santa feels, don't I?"

Bri put her arms out to Brian to be picked up. He scooped her into his arms and laughed.

"What about the furniture and the Christmas trees?" Ellen asked. "It's too perfect. Was it already like this?"

"I had Biltmore rent the furniture for me," Brian said. "And the kids stayed behind to decorate the trees. They bought the decorations and everything."

"Well, not all of us helped," Lane admitted. "Maya and I spent the day with her parents."

"We had fun doing it," Taylor said. "Didn't we?"

"Absolutely," Nolan said with a hint of sarcasm.

"The look on your faces was the best gift ever," Alison said.

"I wish you could have seen it," Luke said.

"I caught it on video on my camera," Mike said. "I'll share it with y'all."

"Great idea," Lexi said. "I can't wait to see it."

"I hope you're hungry," Nolan said.

"The catering is from Hemingway's Cuba," Maya said. "It's my parents' favorite place."

"The food is Cuban," Lane added. "I hope everyone likes it."

"It smells fabulous," Sue said.

"Then why don't we eat?" Dave suggested.

As they formed two lines around the buffet table, Sue said, "By the way, Nolan was right. My kneecap isn't broken. I'm so relieved."

"So am I," Tom said.

"Only because now you're off the hook," Sue teased.

"I don't know what you mean," Tom said as he waited in line to fill his plate. "I'm never off the hook when it comes to you."

"True," Sue said with a laugh. She took his hand and kissed the back of it.

"No making out in the ballroom," Tanya teased.

Once their plates were filled with beef and chicken empanadas, smoked ham croquettes, sirloin steak, black beans, rice, and fried plantains, each family sat together at their respective tables to eat and visit. Ellen couldn't be more pleased with the food or the conversation. It was more relaxing than it had been at the wedding. When they'd finished, they retreated to their sitting areas with churros to open their gifts.

Ellen was grateful for the opportunity to see the expressions on her loved ones' faces when they unwrapped their presents from her and Brian. She was especially pleased when Bri opened her motorized Barbie car. She climbed in behind the wheel and was ready to drive.

"This is perfect for her," Nolan said. "Thanks, Mom and Brian."

"It barely fit in the jet," Brian said with a laugh.

"I'm so glad you didn't get her anything that beeps or sings," Taylor said. "I think my parents bought gifts to test our wits."

"Well, she'll keep you on your toes with this Barbie car," Ellen said. "There's no rest until they're twenty-one."

"So we've been told," Nolan said as he chased Bri in her car around the room.

"And this is for you," Brian said, handing Ellen a small, wrapped box.

She opened his gift to find a beautiful pendant and matching earrings with black gemstones in silver settings.

"They're gorgeous," she said. "Thank you so much."

"They're tourmaline," he said. "When you told me that tourmaline protects you from spiritual attacks, I wanted to cover you with it. I wanted a tourmaline *coat* to wrap you in but couldn't find one."

"But I only just told you about the tourmaline yesterday," she said.

"I've got friends in high places," he said with a grin.

Ellen laughed. "Oh, Brian. I'm so grateful for you." She threw her arms around his neck. "My gift won't seem like much in comparison."

"I'm sure I'll love it no matter what it is," he said as she handed him a card.

He opened it, read it, and arched a brow. "Golf lessons?"

"I'm really sorry, darling, but Tom and Mike say you aren't very good."

He threw back his lead and laughed.

Later that night, alone in their room together at Biltmore Inn, as they readied for bed, Ellen said to Brian, "From now on you'll be forever known as the man who saved Christmas."

"I like the sound of that," he said as he turned out the bathroom light.

She threw her arms around his neck, "Well, I like the sound of you."

He pressed his lips hard against hers, and she swooned against him, feeling young, vibrant, and happy.

As they pulled back the covers and climbed into bed, she said, "I was just telling Sue and Tanya that turning sixty's not so bad."

He cupped her face and grinned. "No, it's not so bad at all."

CHAPTER TWENTY-THREE

Loose Ends

The Dining Room at the Biltmore Inn reminded Ellen of the Vanderbilt Ballroom with its ivory coffered ceiling and its red and gold classically patterned carpeting. Like the ballroom, it had candelabra chandeliers and a stone fireplace with a wooden mantle and a crackling fire in the hearth. The mantle was decorated for Christmas with fir garlands and pinecones, and a large wreath hung above. The tables were covered in white linens, fine china, and glassware, and the wooden chairs were upholstered with gold damask fabric.

Ellen, Sue, and Tanya sat at a table for four waiting for Linda Bracken, whom Ellen had invited to join them for dinner. Sue was walking with a cane now and was seated in a regular chair at the table, though they had brought the old-fashioned wheelchair to return to Linda.

Ellen took a sip of her Chardonnay. "I hope she's made some progress."

"We're about to find out," Sue said. "Here she comes."

"I'm sorry I'm late," Linda said as she took her seat. "I ran home to change after my shift and got caught in traffic."

"No worries," Ellen said. "It gave us time to share a bottle of Biltmore wine."

"And what did you think of it?" Linda asked.

"It's delicious," Sue said. "Would you like a glass?"

"Absolutely," Linda said.

Sue poured the last of their bottle into a glass for Linda.

"Thanks." Linda took a sip.

They looked over their menus.

"I think I'm getting the same thing I've had every night since we checked in," Sue said. "I can't get enough of their pecan crusted salmon."

"That's not very adventurous," Tanya said.

"Look where being adventurous has got me," Sue said.

"I mean with the food," Tanya said. "I'm going to try the sweet potato gnocchi."

"It's my favorite dish," Linda said. "I'm a vegetarian, so my choices are limited. But even my non-vegetarian friends have said it's their favorite thing on the menu."

"Well, I'm having the chicken roulade," Ellen said. "I've been wanting to try it."

After they gave their order to the server, Ellen asked Linda, "Have you made any progress with your efforts to exonerate your grandfather?"

"Oh, yes," Linda said. "It turns out that one of my colleagues is a big Gallatin Roberts fan. He already believed my grandfather was innocent without having ever read the diaries."

"And is he going to help you?" Sue asked.

"He already has," Linda said. "He convinced the owners to allow us to put up a display dedicated to my grandfather. He was the very first guest on the registry, after the house was opened to the public. Did you know that?"

Ellen lifted her brows. "So that's what he meant."

"What?" Tanya asked.

"He told me that, but I thought he meant on Lane and Maya's registry. I even went to look, but the first on their registry was Sue and Tom."

"Now you know," Sue said.

Linda took a sip of her wine. "It's still so hard to believe. You must excuse my incredulity."

"It takes some getting used to," Ellen said.

"Ellen should know," Sue said. "She was a greater skeptic than you not more than five years ago."

Ellen blushed. "That's true."

"So, Linda, will this display honoring your grandfather mention anything about his innocence?" Sue asked.

"Until we get the courts to agree to his innocence, we're going to word it like this: 'Although he and six other officials were indicted for malfeasance in February 1931, authorities found nothing but circumstantial evidence, and since then other information casts significant doubt on his guilt.'"

"That sounds perfect for now," Ellen said. "Oh, he should be so relieved."

"I hope so," Linda said.

The server arrived with their first course. Ellen and Tanya had the crab soup, Sue had the crab cake, and Linda had the squash and pumpernickel crisp.

As they ate, Linda said, "It's interesting that of all the ghosts that might have been haunting Biltmore, it was my grandfather. It's not like he died there or spent much time there."

"He probably followed his trunk," Sue said.

"We spoke to two other ghosts who were less tied to the estate than he was," Ellen pointed out.

"Oh? Who?"

Ellen and her friends told Linda about Melinda Brown and Zelda Fitzgerald. They also told her about the reconciliation that took place between the two sets of grandparents.

"I'm a big fan of Zelda Fitzgerald," Linda said just as their server brough their entrees.

"Really?" Tanya asked. "How so?"

"I've written many articles about historical Asheville, and my piece covering Zelda's death is one of the most memorable."

"I can imagine," Sue said.

"Did you happen to visit Grove Park Inn before you came to Biltmore?" Linda asked.

"As a matter of fact, we did," Ellen said. "We stayed there our first night here."

"You do know that her husband Scott stayed there quite often to write," Linda said. "And Zelda would visit him there whenever the doctors at Highland Hospital would allow it."

"No, we didn't know that," Sue said.

"I'm telling you this because it's possible that Zelda followed you to Biltmore from Grove Park Inn. I never paid much attention to it, but people have claimed to see her there in her pink tutu."

Ellen lifted her brows and glanced at her friends. "I suppose that's possible."

"What really matters," Tanya said, "is that we try our best to help her to rest. She's been in a kind of hell for so long. It's made her vindictive. Evil."

"We're worried she could bring harm to others," Ellen explained.

"I guess Zelda doesn't know that historians are already aware that Scott plagiarized her," Linda said before taking another sip of her wine. "I'm not sure how you can convince her."

"I just had an idea," Ellen said suddenly. "Do you think the Biltmore people would be open to creating a display for her, like the one you're making for your grandfather? Maybe it could be on a side table in the music room—just a photo and an explanation of her unacknowledged contributions to American literature."

"That's a great idea," Tanya said.

"But would Biltmore go for it?" Sue asked.

"I think they would," Linda said. "The owners are fans of Fitzgerald's works. That's why they're in the library to begin with. I think this would fascinate them. They're always looking for ways to inject more history into the tour."

Ellen clapped her hands together. "Wonderful. This may be the very thing to help her to cross over."

"That is, if she doesn't kill us first," Sue said.

The next day at dusk, Ellen, Sue, and Tanya met Shiri on the front lawn near the fountain at Biltmore House. Although the moon was a waning gibbous, it still appeared partially full and bright—bright enough to see the grass at their feet and the house in the distance. No traces of snow remained. The air was chilly but not freezing. Sue, who was still using her cane, sat on the stone lip that encircled the fountain, next to seven crystals Shiri had laid out.

"What if the spirits don't come?" Tanya asked after they'd greeted Shiri, who had been waiting there for them.

Most of the tourists had gone, but not all. Ellen wondered if any of them had the slightest idea of why the four of them had gathered there on the lawn.

"I have a way of attracting them," Shiri said. "It just takes time."

"Or, what if they come," Sue began, "but Zelda tries to kill us again."

"I brought protection," Shiri said.

"The last boy who told me that was lying," Sue said in a teasing tone.

"I'll bathe us in sage smoke first." Shiri lit the end of a smudge stick and blew on it until the flame went out and the smoke began to curl up into the air.

One at a time, Shiri bathed them in the smoke while saying, "I use this sage to create a barrier of protection from negative energy. Nothing negative or evil is allowed to break through. I call upon the elements of earth, fire, water, and air to help us."

"Oh, that's why you had us meet at the fountain," Ellen surmised.

"Exactly," Shiri said.

When she had finished smudging, Shiri dipped the smoking end into the fountain, to fully extinguish it before lying it on the stone lip next to Sue and her crystals.

"Each one of these stones serves a purpose," Shiri explained. She picked up a gray stone with a marbled texture that sparkled in the moonlight. "This first one is labradorite. Some people believe it was formed when the Northern Lights were trapped in ice. It's known for stimulating the crown and third eye chakras. It possesses a highly tuned vibration that makes it easier to pass freely between the spiritual and physical planes."

"What's it called again?" Sue asked.

"Labradorite," Shiri said as she put it down and picked up the next stone—which was a deeper gray than the other, closer to black. "This is smokey quartz. It aids in helping you to find spirits you want to talk to, while it also protects us by absorbing any negative energy that might threaten us."

"Smokey quartz," Sue repeated.

Shiri put down the quartz and picked up the third stone—a deep olive green. "This is moldavite. It's a crystal that came from a meteorite that landed in Moldova, Russia over 14.8 million years ago."

"Wow. Is it rare?" Tanya asked.

"Somewhat. It's my favorite because it opens all the chakras and magnifies a witch's talents. It also is a connector to the spiritual realm, making crossovers and banishments easier to perform."

"That's good to know," Sue said.

"This is selenite," Shiri said as she picked up the white stone. "It's a crystal the ancient Greeks named after Selene, the moon goddess. It opens the channels between the spiritual and physical worlds, so it's perfect for our purposes tonight."

Shiri returned the selenite to the lip of the fountain and picked up the cobalt blue one beside it. "This is lapis-lazuli. It attracts spirits while protecting us from psychic attacks. It also opens all chakras, mainly the heart, throat, and third eye. It increases our psychic powers and helps us to keep control over unruly spirits."

"I've always likes lapis-lazuli," Tanya said. "Now I like it even more."

Shiri returned the cobalt blue stone to the lip of the fountain and picked up the red one. "This is red jasper. It will keep us grounded by opening our root chakra. This protects us from psychic manipulation."

"It's pretty, too," Sue said.

"These gemstones are like us," Ellen said with a smile. "They're beautiful and powerful."

"Exactly," Shiri said, as she set down the red jasper and picked up the final stone. It was pink. "This is watermelon tourmaline. It's rare and another of my favorites because it protects us from psychic attacks but also attracts spirits, especially those that are hard to find."

"With this arsenal, how can we go wrong?" Ellen said optimistically.

"Confidence is good," Shiri said as she lit a candle and placed it near the stones. "But don't let your guard down. Be ready for anything."

"This may sound like a stupid question," Ellen began, "but what exactly is a chakra?"

"They talk about them in my yoga class," Tanya said. "Aren't they centers of energy in the body?"

"Yes, that's right," Shiri said. "And they're responsible for different aspects of our physical and spiritual wellbeing. A blocked chakra can cause health problems. An open chakra is better for you."

"How does a chakra become blocked?" Tanya asked.

"Too much stress. Trauma. Negative energy." Shiri opened her palms toward the night sky. "Are we ready to begin?"

"Shouldn't we make a circle of protection with salt?" Sue asked.

"These crystals serve the same purpose," Shiri said, "but if you have salt, it wouldn't hurt."

"After what we experienced in the Biltmore House, I vote for using the salt," Tanya said.

"Me, too," Ellen agreed.

Sue pulled a shaker from her purse and handed it to Tanya, who then sprinkled it in the grass in a counterclockwise motion. When she reached the lip of the fountain, she was careful to include the candle, the crystals, and Sue inside the ring.

"Okay," Tanya said as she returned the shaker to Sue. "Now we're ready."

Shiri lifted her palms toward the night sky. "I call upon my spirit guides to help me tonight, as I and three friends attempt to help three lost souls to find their way home."

Shiri closed her eyes and breathed deeply. "I ground myself to the earth and to the physical realm as I call upon my spirit guides for help. And now, we will name those lost souls we wish to aid."

Shiri nodded to Sue, who said, "Melinda Brown."

She nodded at Tanya, who said, "Gallatin Roberts."

Then she nodded at Sue, who said, "Zelda Fitzgerald."

"We seek your permission to help you to find peace and contentment. We want you to join the divine light, to become part of the divine body, and to leave your troubles behind."

Shiri's eyes suddenly widened.

"Do you sense something?" Ellen whispered.

"They're here," she said. "All three of them. There are others, too, but they're in the background, watching. They're curious. I don't know if they need our help."

"Hello," Ellen said lifting her hands in the air. "We're here to help."

"We have good news for all three of you," Sue added. "Melinda Brown, your sister told the truth to Ted, and both couples are friends again."

"She's smiling," Shiri said. "And now she's weeping, but I think they're happy tears."

"Melinda? Are you ready to cross over into the light?" Ellen asked. "Can you see any of your other departed loved ones waiting for you on the other side?"

"She says if the moon were full, you would see her," Shiri said. "She wishes you could see her one more time before she goes."

"Tell her we just want her to find peace," Tanya said. "That's why we do what we do. We mean to help, to heal."

"She's crossed over," Shiri said. "Another woman came and took her hand and led her over. There are others lingering near the portal. Dozens of spirits from the other side have come to help. I don't know who they are. They aren't speaking to me."

"Gallatin Roberts?" Ellen began. "Did you know that Biltmore House is making a display that will exonerate you to millions of visitors each year? And your granddaughter is going to work through the courts to get your indictment overturned."

"He's nodding and smiling," Shiri said. "He says to thank you. Wow."

"What?" Tanya asked.

"He has so many people waiting for him, helping him. They are all weeping. They've longed for this moment to have him home."

Tears sprang to Ellen's eyes. "Oh, how beautiful."

"What about Zelda?" Sue asked. "Are you ready to cross over? Don't you want to see your daughter and mother and sisters?"

"The ballerina is shaking her head. She wants to know if you've exonerated her."

"Sue published her article about you," Ellen said, "and one of the docents here is working with the people at Biltmore to get a display honoring you and educating their visitors about your contributions to American literature. Linda Bracken, the docent, told us that the historians already know that your husband plagiarized you. So, now we just need to make it public knowledge, and Linda is sure that Biltmore will help."

"She seems uncertain," Shiri said. "I don't know if she'll accept the help of those on the other side. They are reaching out to her, but she isn't going with them."

"You don't have to go," Sue said, "but I think you'll be happier if you do. Don't you want to let go of the pain and misery that has tethered you here?"

"She's nodding," Shiri said. "But she continues to ignore those calling to her."

"Those are your loved ones," Ellen said to Zelda. "They miss you and long to be with you. Can't you accept their offers of love and companionship?"

"She's glancing behind her, at those calling to her," Shiri said. "She's still hesitating, though."

"I promise you, Zelda," Ellen said. "I promise that the living will know the truth. You can trust us. Let go of your anger. Let go of your disappointment. Let go of your despair. Accept love. Accept light. Accept companionship. Accept joy by going with your loved ones and embracing eternal peace."

"She's nodding," Shiri said. "She just curtseyed and said thank you and goodbye. She's taking the hands of a female spirit. She's kissing her cheek and calling her Scottie. And now she's hugging her mother and squeezing the hands of—I think they're her sisters. She's saying their names: Tilde, Rosalind, and Marjory. They are all weeping tears of joy. Oh, Zelda is waving goodbye to us."

Shiri waved.

"Where is she?" Ellen asked.

"There." Shiri pointed toward the moon.

Ellen, Tanya, and Sue waved goodbye to Zelda.

"We forgive you," Ellen said, not so much for Zelda's sake as for her own. "We forgive you, and we wish you peace."

During the flight back, Tanya, who had the aisle seat beside Ellen, looked up from her phone and said, "I've been thinking about my sixtieth birthday."

"Birthdays aren't as much fun when you're older," Sue said from the window seat. "But fortunately, you don't have as many more to go."

"I'd watch what I say if I were you," Ellen said. "You're not far behind."

"I know. I'm only teasing. So, tell us, Tanya, what have you been thinking?"

"I've been trying to think of something memorable to do, and I've just figured it out."

"Well?" Sue asked.

"I want to take a *Twilight* tour in Forks, Washington," she said. "Remember when we used to have our book club, how much we all loved *Twilight?* I've watched the movies at least a dozen times."

"I have, too," Ellen admitted. "Alison got me into them. It's something we like to do together."

"La Push Beach is not far from Forks, just like in the books," Tanya said. "And according to this website, there's a bungalow on the Quileute reservation that the Native Americans can't seem to rent or sell because it's known to be haunted. We should stay there."

"Seriously?" Ellen asked. "This is what you want for your birthday?"

"I'm game," Sue said. "Sounds intriguing."

"Really?" Tanya's face beamed. "What about you, Ellen? Will you go with us?"

"There's no way . . . I'd let you go without me."

The three friends laughed as they began to plan for their next paranormal adventure.

***

THE END

Thank you for reading my story. I hope you enjoyed it! If you did, please consider leaving a review. Reviews help other readers to discover my books, which helps me.

Please visit my website at evapohler.com to get the next book, *A Holiday Haunting at the Biltmore.*

EVA POHLER

Eva Pohler is a *USA Today* bestselling author of over thirty novels in multiple genres, including mysteries, thrillers, and young adult paranormal romance based on Greek mythology. Her books have been described as "addictive" and "sure to thrill"—*Kirkus Reviews*.

To learn more about Eva and her books, and to sign up to hear about new releases, and sales, please visit her website at https://www.evapohler.com.